D1753523

The Sky Hangs Low

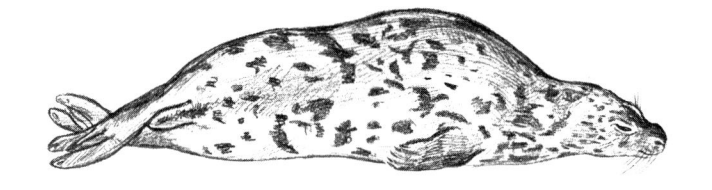

The Sky Hangs Low

Original text and drawings by Jens Rosing

Translated from the Danish by Naomi Jackson Groves

Penumbra Press

Copyright © Jens Rosing, Naomi Jackson Groves, 1986.

Published by PENUMBRA PRESS, P.O. Box 340, Moonbeam, Ontario, Canada POL 1VO.

Original Danish edition published by Wormianum, Aarhus, 1979.

The text is set in Aldus by the Coach House Press (Toronto). Printed and bound by the Porcupine's Quill (Erin). Stock is 100 lb. Plainfield Offset and 10 pt. Cornwall Cover.

ISBN 0 920806 86 4

CONTENTS

Translator's Introduction 6

The Graves Under the Rock 9

The Dead 24

The Eskimos' Clothing 38

Biographical Details 58

Translator's Introduction

IT WAS THE ALMOST indescribable impact of the small face of a six-month-old dead Inuit baby that I first saw on the cover of a little magazine named *Skalk* (Volume 6, 1978) in Denmark in June 1983, when I was gathering material before taking a group of friends and relatives to visit Greenland in August, which continued to haunt me from then on, and has now led to this translation of the book that tells about that baby and its family. The little head and body, still so appealing in the furry hooded jacket, are the real, actually 'existent' remains of a small child who was alive and kicking at the time Leonardo da Vinci was that same age – the latter born in A.D. 1452, over five hundred years ago. Modern carbon dating for the Inuit baby shows '1460, give or take forty or fifty years each way.'

The baby belongs to a group of Thule Eskimos who lived half way up the west coast of Greenland, near Umanaq Island with its towering conical mountain. The infant was found with seven other members of that family group (relationships for three generations were established by comparing samples of the 500-year-old muscle tissues still present in the various bodies, the white corpuscles usually tested no longer being available ...). Most, if not all, of the eight must have died a sudden death from some disastrous accident, likely drowning when their skin-covered umiak was swamped offshore. All the adults in the group are women, all clad in their fur and birdskin clothing which has remained incredibly intact, by and large, providing well-preserved examples about two hundred years older than any other Inuit costumes found in the anthropologists' treasure-house of Greenland.

The six women and two children, the baby and an older boy of about four years of age (lacking two front baby teeth which had fallen out before death), must have been carefully laid to rest by the loving and grieving survivors, their menfolk, who wrapped them in extra furs and laid heather twigs and dried grass under and around them to soften the hard stone of the crevice up the mountain-side high above their tiny settlement, which at that time consisted of two turf houses for at most five families. The bodies, protected under an overhang, must have frozen very soon afterward and scarcely deteriorated since then, many of their garments hardly at all, except for drying out. The eight were there when Columbus came across, and had been lying there already for two hundred years when Rembrandt was painting in Holland (he would have liked them too).

Why – some of us may wish, and ask – could they not have been left there for many centuries more, where they 'belonged'? It is a highly regrettable but inescapable fact that, due to the present-day accessibility of the once remote Greenland coast, casual tourist visitors now prowl about, 'collecting' ancient artifacts, specimens of clothing, 'old bones', to carry off as souvenirs to their distant homelands. So in our modern, highly advanced scientific age, modern Greenlanders are no longer able to allow their interesting ancestors to rest in peace up on the mountain-side.

The reference to the dead bodies as 'mummies' in this book, is in a sense misleading, as they are not in the least 'fixed up' or embalmed, merely desiccated by natural conditions. The Greenland-born Jens Rosing, author as well of that first article which 'hooked' me in June 1983, was Director of the Greenland Museum in Godthåb (now usually called Nuuk) in November 1977. That was when the first finder of the ancient grave site, a native of nearby Umanaq, brought in some photos a friend had taken for him, without disturbing the bodies. Jens Rosing quickly had the right professional help sent out from Copenhagen, and he was present when the stones were permanently lifted from above the bodies in 1978, so that they could be taken to Copenhagen for full scientific examination.

His vivid, play-by-play descriptions of the first appearance of the bodies in their resting-place, as well as his further details about the 'people' (which is the literal translation of the term *Inuit*, singular *Inuk*), their homes, their way of life and their beliefs, are lively and sensitive, as well as scientifically based. He was, in my opinion, fully justified at that early stage in allowing his native insight and imaginative sense of 'rightness' – the leap of faith of the artist's instinct – to make certain assumptions into the cause of death of so many people in the same grave: people who, he soon learned from Copenhagen, all 'carbon dated' to the same death-date (give or take those forty years) and for almost all of whom vast amounts of later scientific museum research have not been able to find other reasons for death, such as physical violence or problems of health. Nor can any other satisfactory explanation be found why, apart from the two children clad in boys' costume, it is only women who are there, without any of the usual 'grave gifts' of their household implements of stone and bone, which may well be resting deep in the cold sea outside Qilakitsoq.

Jens Rosing's own pen-and-ink drawings and watercolours also give this work a compelling immediacy. I know that my group of twenty-four who visited Greenland in August 1983 and hung over the glass case in which the baby and several other family members were being shown in Godthåb Museum, shared the amazement and fascination I was feeling, and which I now hope this book will convey to others as well.

SINCE MY INTEREST in this project began, at least two popular publications have been brought forth in richly colour-embellished formats. First was *The Sunday Times Magazine*, April 25, 1984, with Inuit baby's photo in colour on the full front page: 'The baby who lived 500 years ago. First dramatic pictures of the 15th century family preserved in an Arctic tomb.' Inside, in almost seven full pages with colour spreads, Kenneth Pearson reports on 'The family that came in from the cold.' Second was an article 'The Mummies of Qilakitsoq,' by Jens P. Hart Hansen, Chief of Pathology at Gentofte Hospital in Denmark, Jørgen Meldgaard,

Chief Curator of the Inuit Collection at the National Museum, and Jørgen Nordqvist, Chief of the Archaeological Conservation Department of the Museum, in the *National Geographic* for February 1985, pages 190 to 207, with photos of the bodies stretched out for clinical examination, their hands (covered with a white fungus and then cleaned), their clothing, the best of it cleaned up and very stylish, etc.

The same three were authors of the 'big' popular-science type book in Danish, *Qilakitsoq*, Christian Ejlers' Forlag, Copenhagen, 1985, full of detailed findings by about fifty different scientists, all of whom neglect to mention Jens Rosing's name in their text, let alone the fact that he had already contributed two publications on the subject. There is a brief word of thanks to him in the foreword by the Greenland cultural authorities for the fact that he 'arranged for the undertaking of the project, which can now be presented in book form.' The lengthy bibliography at the end merely gives his name and title of *Himlen er lav*, Aarhus 1979. The 'big' book now in Danish will presumably be followed by translations in other languages. It is to be hoped that Jens Rosing's initial concept will continue to carry its own weight, as well as far more poetic punch than anything else I have seen so far.

In June 1985, once again in Denmark, I had the great pleasure of meeting Jens Rosing in person, and of visiting his fascinating home on the outskirts of the town of Humlebaek, which lies not far from Elsinore in northern Sjaelland and is site of the celebrated modern art collection, Louisiana. After meeting Rosing, I came away feeling admiration, respect and sincere affection for the artist-author, who is a prime living example of those *Doppelbegabungen*, doubly-gifted, many-sided creative artists whom I have been writing about for quite a long time now. Other publications by Rosing have provided fine details which I happily include, at the end, as added enrichment. In return, Jens Rosing's own 'Postscript' that ended *Himlen er lav* in 1979 can be dispensed with, as it merely mentions the types of scientific work that would be underway at the National Museum before the bodies could be returned to Greenland. When later established accuracies seem to be pertinent to Rosing's 1978 / 79 text, I have occasionally inserted them in square brackets prefaced by 'NOTE:' – and once in a while accompanied by my responsible initials, NJG.

May I express my grateful thanks for good friends' help, both in Denmark and here in Canada.

Naomi Jackson Groves
Ottawa, 1986

The Graves Under the Rock

QILAKITSOQ is the Greenlandic name of an ancient settlement on the north side of the Nugssuaq peninsula seven kilometres from Umanaq in West Greenland. According to an old report on the district, this location has not been inhabited since the 1780s, and it remains deserted, although it is visited in summer by fishermen and in winter by ptarmigan hunters. But there is clear evidence that the place had before that time been home for small communities during at least two thousand years: traces of the old houses can still be clearly seen in the terrain.

This was the peaceful spot to which the brothers Hans and Jokum Grønvold came in by boat one autumn day in 1972, in order to hunt for ptarmigan in the mountains at Qilakitsoq. On arrival they separated and each took his own route. Hans waded through the snow up over a steep stony stretch towards an overhanging rock about fifty metres from the coast. He knew from previous hunting trips that there was a spot where snow never remains on the ground, a good place to rest, with a fine view out across a wide expanse of fjord and land.

While Hans stood there he noticed a striking difference in the rock material below the overhang. The ground looked as if it were levelled with stone fragments brought from some other place. On closer examination it became evident that the fragments were covering several large flat stones, and through a crack he saw a hollow space beneath. Down there in the dark he could dimly discern something that looked almost like a bundle of leather crushed together.

Now Jokum arrived and together they removed some of the rock fragments so that a covering stone could be moved. Out from a large bundle of furs protruded a pair of kamiks (Eskimo sealskin

Protruding rock under which the graves lay, seen from the east.

boots), and when the brothers carefully lifted the furs the bodies of two children came into view, both totally desiccated, and clad in well-preserved skin outfits. The larger child, a boy, had the hood of his jacket up around his head, and on his legs the aforementioned kamiks, with unusually fine-sewed soles. Lying across him the baby rested, face down, likewise with its hood pulled well forward to cover its ears. In addition, it wore a pair of 'kick-pants' or leggings, with stockings and pants in one piece, made of soft animal skin with the fur side inward.

The 6 to 7 year-old boy. [Note: Bone structure shows him to be only 4.]

The baby boy.

But there were more people still. Under the children lay a tall woman, with the older child's head resting in her lap, and underneath her could be glimpsed the tips of another pair of kamiks. At the very bottom could be seen a bundle – a body enveloped in a great many furs. In all, five human beings.

Nor was that all. A short distance away, only a little over a metre from the front or head end of the grave, the brothers found another grave. This lay at right angles to the first, and revealed, when opened, a similar scene. As far as they could make out, there were three bodies in this one.

It was clear to Hans and Jokum that these dead persons were not of small build, according to today's standards; indeed the woman uppermost in the first grave seemed remarkably tall. They most sensibly left everything untouched, covered the site again and went away. All that they took with them as evidence were one or two articles of clothing, a kamik and a pair of light indoor pants which lay on top of the tall woman. Unfortunately, these bits of clothing suffered the sad fate of being thrown out during the very first winter, by the young men's father, who was afraid of ghosts and sorcery. But already by that time they had fortunately been shown to people properly concerned with such objects.

The very next day after their discovery, October 10, 1972, the Grønvold brothers reported their find to the communal authorities in Umanaq. A detailed telegram was sent to the Greenland Museum in Godthåb. In it was reported that a total of eight human bodies lay under the rocky overhang. The matter awakened a good deal of attention and the find was reported on Greenland

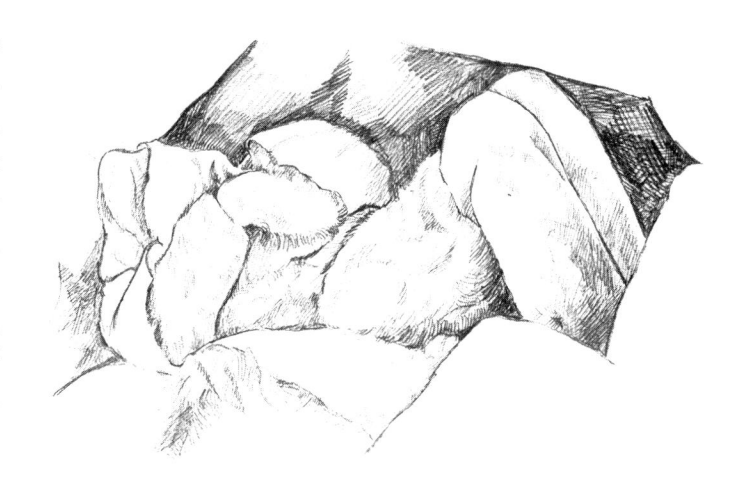

The top body in Grave 2 as it looked when the fur rug was removed.

Radio; then nothing more happened on that round. At that stage conditions for the museums in Greenland were chaotic, and several other aspects likely contributed to the matter not being followed up at the time.

That this unique discovery remained as 'untouched' as it did, and not disturbed by persons it did not concern, is due to the two Grønvold brothers. They were fully conscious of the importance of their find, and shut up like clams when their report did not lead to a follow-up examination. Only a couple of close friends were allowed to look at their find, when the site was visited with them and some photographs were taken. With these in hand Jokum Grønvold visited me in November 1977 in my office in Godthåb, where I had meanwhile become Museum Director.

The pictures were so convincing that the matter was followed up speedily. From the Greenland Museum a message went to the National Museum in Copenhagen with the request to be allowed to 'borrow' Conservator Gerda Møller for at least a period of time at Easter 1978.

Thanks to the favour of the weather gods, we were able to step out of our helicopter from Søndre Strømfjord (Southern Stream-fjord) in Umanaq on Good Friday, 1978. It was fine weather with the sun riding high, and the air was so cold that it glittered with frost crystals. The sledding was fantastically good; the dogs fanned the traces wide and dashed along. This was North Greenland.

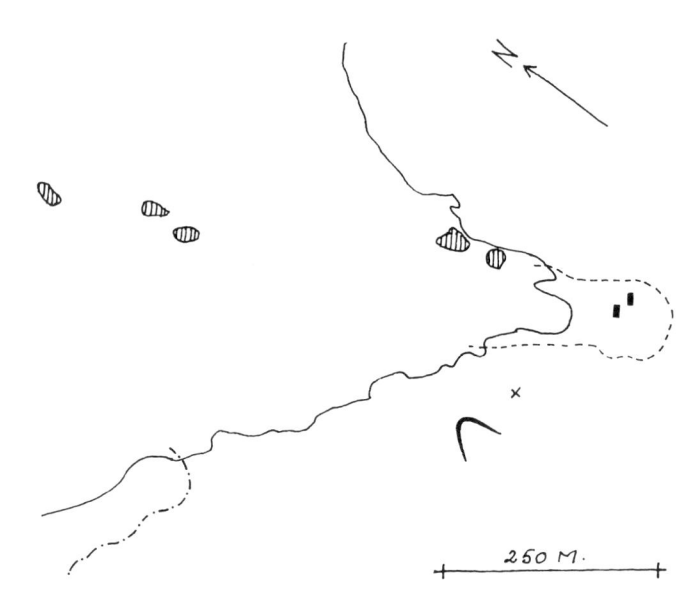

Qilakitsoq. The dotted line indicates the settlement area and shows at the same time where the steep rocky mountain cliffs rise around the dwelling area. Only the two most visible house sites are shown. Out in the fjord the skerries which appear at low tide are shown in cross hatching. The lookout point is shown by a cross. The heavily printed curve shows the contour of the rocky overhang under which the graves lay. The line and dot contour shows the tenting area to which people moved in springtime.

On Easter Sunday the business manager of the district, Sven Gjerulf, with Jokum Grønvold as guide, drove us by jeep across to Nugssuaq. The snow on the fjord ice was only about 10 centimetres deep.

After considerable wading through snow which covered the track up the mountainside, we arrived under the projecting rock where the graves lay. It was unusually cold up there, as the place lay in shadow. After our combined efforts had moved the covering stones to one side, we were treated to a sight which corresponded exactly to the information the two brothers had given us, as already described.

The location where the burial place lies is named ét Alańgoq – shadow or shaded side. Qilakitsoq – the place with the low sky – is a small bay opening to the west, ringed on three sides by steep mountains. When you stand at the centre of the settlement space, and gaze up at the 500-metre high mountain ridge to the east and the south, your neck must be bent away back, and all you can see is a dark, steep mountain wall and a tiny strip of sky. Hence its name. The old name-givers were certainly right: the heavens hang low over this dwelling-place.

The old Qilakitsoq settlement lay a little over 200 metres, as the crow flies, from the grave site. As mentioned earlier, the area has not been inhabited since the end of the 1700s, as proved by the ruins of houses, of which two large ones are clearly visible in the present-day landscape. The house farthest from the shore is a 'row house' with three rooms separated by two entrance passages. The rooms themselves were each not larger than 4 x 4 metres, and the entire ruin is 12 x 15 metres in

Front view of the Qilakitsoq house which lies farthest from the shore. The division of the rooms can be seen from the flat stones which hold the turf walls in place. In both this and the other houses, these stones follow the curve of the walls underneath the roof turfs. Due to lack of wood, the roof construction was extremely narrow. Tent poles, umiak boat oars and bones of large sea mammals served as rafters and lathes. The builders counted upon the slabs of turf freezing together rapidly, and no one was allowed to walk on the roof top. The window panes are strips of animal intestine sewed together; they can be installed in grooves above the entrance passages, held by narrow strips of wood or framed in solid strips of hide wedged firmly into the turf wall. The entire length of the house must have been 12-15 metres.

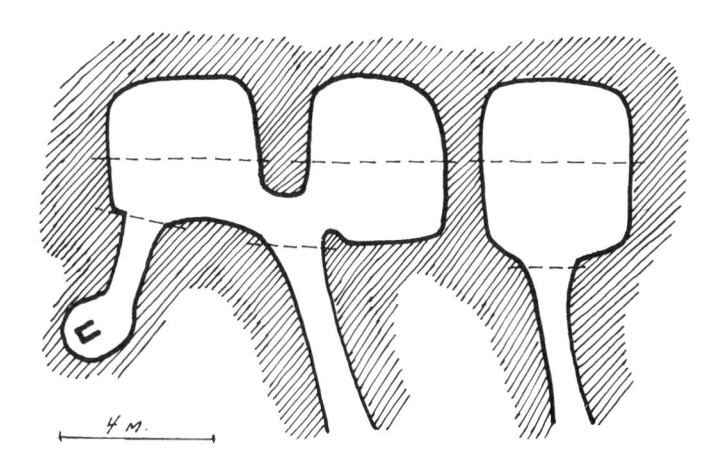

Ground plan of the same house. The dotted lines indicate the edge of the sleeping platform and the entrance threshold. When the family moves in, the platform is covered with branches of heather and furs, and fur hides are hung along the walls. The house floor and passages are paved with flat stones. To the left can be seen the cooking recess, which is connected with its room by a sunken passage about 3 metres in length. The cooking recess has an open smoke hole in the roof and one or two fireplaces on the floor. The meal used to be cooked in soapstone cooking pots over a fire, and for fuel everything flammable available was used – peat, heather and bones, helped along with blubber or whale oil – the smoke of which must certainly have given off a rather acrid reek. The cooking recess is a tenacious legacy from long-distant forefathers when the blubber lamps were so small that they could be used only for lighting, not for preparing meals. The Qilakitsoq people as a matter of fact had large blubber lamps capable of providing light, general warmth and heat for cooking meals.

Top, water colour. The huge boulder at the lookout point of the Qilakitsoq settlement, seen from the east. It would not be surprising if it had once been a site for making sacrifices.

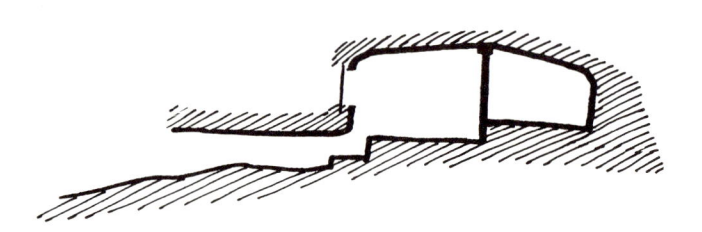

Cross section of the room farthest from the cliffside in the 'row house'. To the right can be seen the post which supports the curve of the roof; it is not over two metres high and is very often a column of stones. To the left is the entrance passage; it is dug down into the ground and so low that one has to bend away down to be able to get through it. Before you can enter the house you have to mount the high threshold which, combined with the sunken passage, prevents the cold air from coming in; this is called the 'cold trap' because the house had no door. If there was need of fresh air, a plug over one of the gutskin window panes was pulled out, allowing air from the cold trap to circulate in the room.

length. This is a type of dwelling that can be dated to the 1400s, and was in use until around 1500, hence the type of house 'our' people lived in, since they, as we shall later see, have been carbon-dated to that period.

Just below this house there lies an equally large one, but in contrast to the first, it has only one large room measuring about 10 x 4 metres, and it has only a single entry passage. This may be Qilakitsoq's last lived-in house, towards the end of the 1700s. Yet there is some evidence that the ground plan for the communal house, as this type is called, was already established in the 1400s. In other words, this house had been modernized later.

Within the settlement's terrain lie several raised mounds that can be interpreted as traces of four other houses.

Closer to the shore, where the turf slope cuts off like a metre-high rampart, there lie remains of even older cultures, namely Sarqaq (at least 3,000

The yellow rock face with opening, exposed by erosion. It lies a little to the west of the Qilakitsoq people's spring camping ground.

years old) and Dorset (at least 2,000 years old). We found stone tools and chips of silicon slate and chalcedony (or agate).

The location has since olden days been a much frequented winter dwelling place. Everywhere along the steep hillside lies grave after grave – some as much as 100 metres up the mountain. [NOTE: The cliffs rise 250 metres high. NJG] We do not know how many graves there may be, but a survey count and a thorough examination would produce several hundred. There were sometimes 3 to 5 skulls and heaps of bones in one and the same grave.

When you visit the settlement in winter, the air feels oppressive, as if the cold were creeping out of all the surrounding cliffs and mountains. It is dark and gloomy. [NOTE: One photo shows low-hanging fog.]

A visit in the autumn makes a milder impression. The grass grows lush and green by the shore and in the settlement area; however, this agreeably mild effect lasts only a short time. As soon as the sun has set and darkness sinks over the landscape, everything seems black, yet the stars shine all the more brilliantly, just like light through a hole in sealskin, as the Eskimos say.

Qilakitsoq, which lies in shadow for most of the year, has had an advantage as far as hunting conditions go, in that the spring and fall migrations of sea mammals, particularly narwhal and white whale, pass close by the bay. Seals and walrus very often enter the bay in their search for food, especially in the fall when the tide keeps the area open longer than the surrounding sea. In spring the same area is more quickly affected by the tide, and the ice breaks up, so that seals and sea birds collect in the open places. The fishing area lies close by in both spring and fall.

Scarcely had spring arrived at the end of April or beginning of May, than the Qilakitsoq inhabitants tore the roof off their winter houses, as the usage was, and raised their tents beside a stretch of

The ice fjord of Qarajak, looking east. Two large glaciers thrust out into the fjord at the right. The place is considered a good breeding area for ring seals.

shoreline where the sun shone long, a little less than a kilometre west of Qilakitsoq. All through the summer they travelled in nomad style from one hunting-ground to another within the complex of the fjord, and finished with the caribou hunt up Nugssuaq's fertile valleys in August and on into September. Toward the end of September they moved back to their winter site.

The climate in Umanaq is the best imaginable, according to arctic standards. Once the ice has formed it is as if the winds freeze away to nothing; day after day in February, March and April there can be brilliant sunshine and 30 to 35 degrees below zero, Celsius. Average annual temperature is minus 6°C and the total precipitation is about 230 mm. As a result there is only up to 10 centimetres of snow on the open stretches of ice, somewhat more in the lee of icebergs and raised ridges of ice. As the ice is solid everywhere and practically unaffected by tidal currents, the district is considered as North Greenland's best area for travel by sled. Seal hunting is generally dependable. Even though klapmyds and Greenland seal can be caught before the ice is solid, the ring seal is beyond comparison the most important of the different species of seal found in the district.

The 71st parallel latitude crosses the middle of the district. The sun disappears on 21 November and reappears on 23 January. The midnight sun shines from 13 May until 31 July.

The most important species of seal in the arctic winter period is the ring seal, *natseq*. The way in which it has adapted itself to ice-covered sea and fjord presented the Inuit with a problem they had to solve in order to survive through the long cold winter. They solved the problem by, among other things, inventing the breathing-hole hunt.

When the fall's thin ice begins to freeze solidly, the ring seal puts his snout up under the ice and blows on it. This forms a hole and the thin broken ice rises over it like a little bell or dome. Without sticking his head up over the ice, the seal dives down and on to another spot where it makes a new hole, and so on. In this way, a system of breathing-holes is formed over a large area of the fjord. On its foraging route all the seal holes are visited and maintained by the breathing of the seal. Ice has been measured up to 2.6 metres thick through which the ring seal has kept the breathing-hole open.

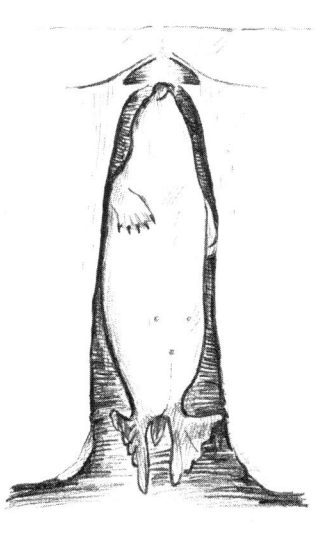

When the ice and snow have increased in depth, one of the holes is widened in the lee of an ice ridge or a small iceberg where the snow has drifted to a firm depth. Here the seal hollows out for itself a snow cave 1½ x 2 metres, where it sleeps and rests in between its hunting expeditions.

Already in March the ring seals can be seen lying upon the ice. They have broken down the snow from over their sleeping hollow and can now enjoy sun and light after the long dark winter. Now the seal is referred to as *utoq*, the one who cooks or who takes a sunbath. In May comes the annual moult for full-grown seals. This lasts ten days and it is a difficult time for the seal; it feels poorly and best likes to lie sleeping on the ice. A seal in its moulting stage is called *marmartoq*, the one who peels off or sheds. Meanwhile the ice evaporates away more and more underneath the seals, and at the same time as the adults get their new coat of fur the ice begins to break up, at the end of May or the beginning of June. Then the young seals move in flocks – from a few up to fifty or so – along the fjord to the outer coast. A new year has begun for the seals, and also for the Inuit.

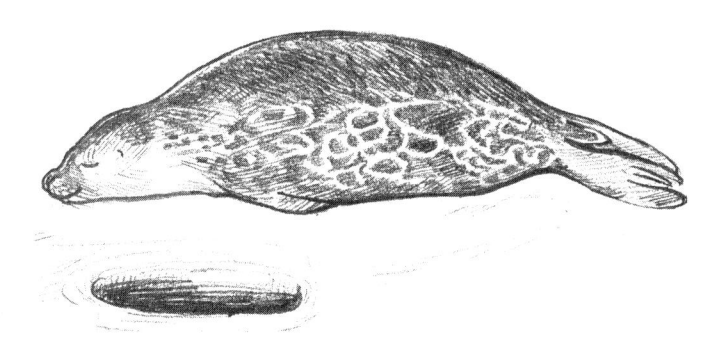

17

In the fall, when the fjord ice has formed during a few days of hard frost, and before another snowfall arrives, the breathing-holes out on the fjord are visited. On still, cold days like this, the seals can be heard breathing.

The hunters divide up around the breathing-holes. Some sit on a hunting chair with their feet on a stool, as shown in the drawing. Others stand in long-furred overshoes pulled on over their kamiks, and wait at the hole. Around each hunter a boy or a woman walks in a wide circle that is gradually narrowed. That is the driver. When a seal is killed it is tied to the ice at the breathing-hole where it was killed, and the hunter goes off to find a new hole. All the going and coming on the ice surface [i.e. disturbing the seals] increases the chances for those who still sit waiting. When darkness comes, the dead seals are pulled up onto the ice and dragged home. An autumn day's hunt on the ice often makes a jolly outing.

But grimly different may be the breathing-hole hunt in the season of darkness, when the area close to the settlement has been hunted empty and the hunter must go farther afield. He now has his dog on a leash. When the dog has sniffed out a breathing-hole, the hunter carefully scrapes away the layer of snow over the breathing-hole, so that the little ice dome is revealed. The hunter settles down on his hunting chair with his feet on the low wooden footstool. His dog lies down a short distance away, and now a long and patient wait begins for man and dog.

Suddenly the hunter senses that the water has risen in the ice tunnel and a gentle gurgling can be heard. In one single movement he bites the glove from his right hand and sets the harpoon point into the shaft, and as he rises he thrusts his weapon violently down into the breathing-hole. If luck is with him, weapon encounters seal just at the ice-crust edge. As a rule the seal is hit so hard that the harpoon point pierces the brain and kills the animal. The dog bounds to its feet.

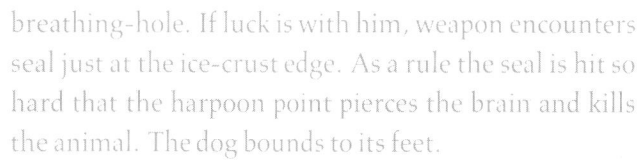

The hunter reverses the harpoon shaft and with its other end, to which an ice chisel of pointed caribou antler has been attached, he widens the opening of the breathing-hole so that it is large enough to drag the seal through. In the course of the harpooning the hunting-line may have been damaged by the crushed skull and may risk being broken in the course of hauling up the animal. The hunter therefore uses a 'hauler' to one end of which a large bone needle has been fastened, to be pushed through the seal's forehead, after which the thong line is pulled halfway through. The hunter takes a firm grip on the thong, pumps the seal up and down in the hole and draws it up onto the ice.

Man and dog help each other to bring home the catch. Very often a hunter and his dog have had to sit and wait for over half a day before the seal makes its presence felt.

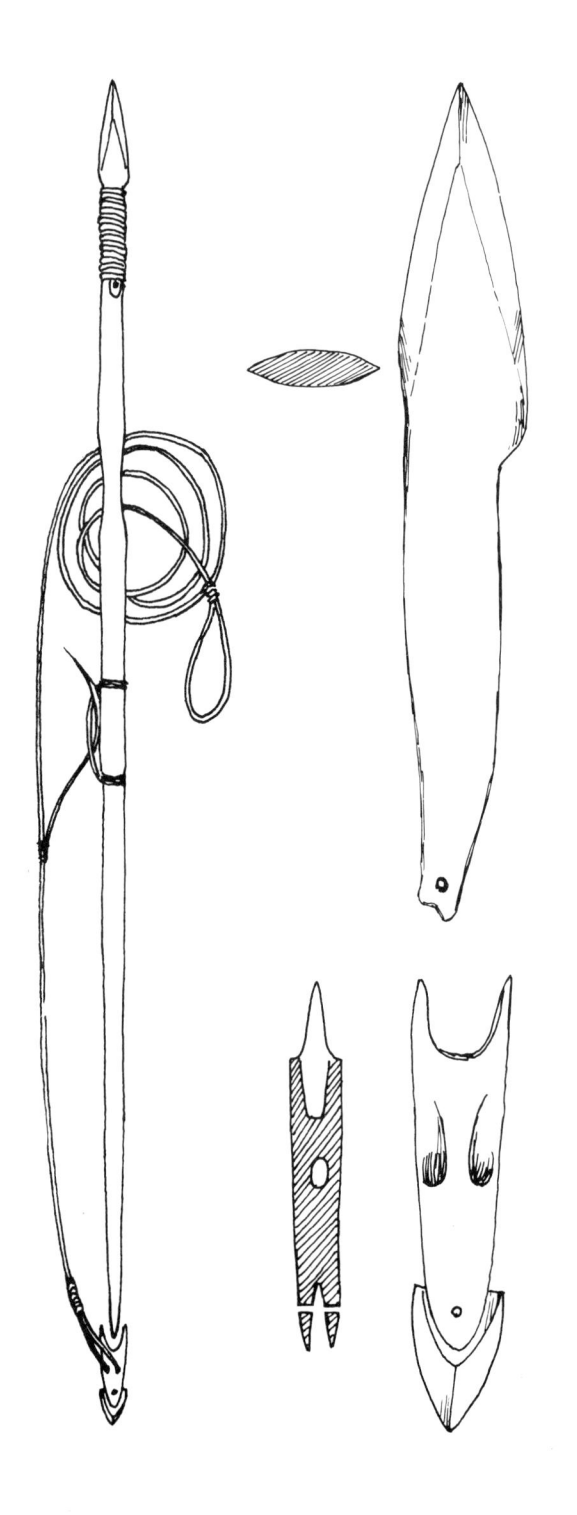

The breathing-hole harpoon. When the weapon is fully mounted, it measures 175 to 180 cm and the thong-line is a good four metres in length. The hunter sticks his hand through the loop at the end of the line so that he has it around his wrist; sometimes a crossbar of bone is used at the end instead. The harpoon shaft itself is of wood.

The ice chisel, *toq*, which is tied firmly to one end of the harpoon shaft, is of caribou antler. The one illustrated here was found in a grave at Kamiorqit on Nugssuaq peninsula, and is 19.5 cm long.

The harpoon point is 7.5 cm long and about 1 cm thick through. The head is of caribou antler and the blade of red-brown slate. From a grave at Ikerasak in Umanaq Fjord.

When the ring seals have reached 3 to 4 years of age the female bears her first pup in March or April. This takes place at the head of the large ice-covered fjords or up an arm of the fjord, and in this area the grown seals remain for the rest of their lives, about 15 to 20 years. When they are full grown they measure 115 to 185 cm from snout to tail-tip, and weigh between 40 and 50 kg, depending on how thick a layer of blubber they have under their skin – there are examples of seals whose half weight consists of blubber. At birth the young seal is 50 to 75 cm long and weighs 10-15 kg, but it gains weight quickly, as its mother's milk contains up to 43% fat and 11% protein; but no lactose. The young seal has whitish yellow fur with a hint of grey along the back. It spends its first weeks in a snow den in the lee of an iceberg where the snow has drifted to some depth. The snow den is as a rule 4 to 5 metres long, but can go up to 10 metres. About four weeks after the birth, the mother leaves the pup in order to mate again – the male seals at this time of the year give off a far-reaching, penetrating odour, and eleven months later the female bears a new offspring. By the time the earlier pup is six weeks old it has changed its white wool costume for a beautiful shining fur coat, and from now on it must fend for itself. Its food consists mainly of shellfish and wing-snails.

The Qilakitsoq people are clothed in fur costumes of young ring seals, as a rule 2 to 3 years old. These are seals which have not yet mated and which roam around from fjord entrances as far as they can under the unmelted fjord ice. A seal at this stage is called *torssusoq*, the long-haired.

The Northern Fulmar (*Mallemukken* – the ice-storm bird) is incontestably Umanaq Fjord's 'national bird'. It arrives at the start of April, while the ice still lies unbroken inside the fjord complex and sled travel is at its height. Every day this outstanding flyer must cover about 80 kilometres from the open sea in Davis Strait in order to attend to its nesting-place on the bird cliffs. One month after arrival the female lays an egg and the pair wait a good 50 days until hatching occurs; then follow 50 days more to feed the young bird, after which the parents leave it to fend for itself from early September on.

There were regularly young northern fulmars in the bay at Qilakitsoq. They pecked around vigorously in the water and it seemed that their favourite prey were wing-snails – in part the uncovered species (in Greenlandic *ataussaq*, the one that looks like the Greenland snail), in part the kind provided with a 'house' or shell, the black wing-snail (*tulugkausaq*), the one who looks like the raven) – that the birds were after. Umanaq in particular is known for the enormous quantity of wing-snails found in the fjords, indeed many kinds of fish, birds and seals get a flavour from them, a rather disagreeable taste. To be sure, the northern fulmar is considered a delicacy among the people of Umanaq, but is eaten most unwillingly in other places.

Among the furs around the dead bodies there lay blue-grey feathers of the northern fulmar.

The ptarmigan, male and female. This is Greenland's only type of everyday poultry; it can be found summer and winter in the Umanaq district. On our first visit at Easter 1978 we saw a small flock of ptarmigan fly up from the cliffside at the burial site. In its winter plumage the ptarmigan may have a faint rosy tinge in its white feathers.

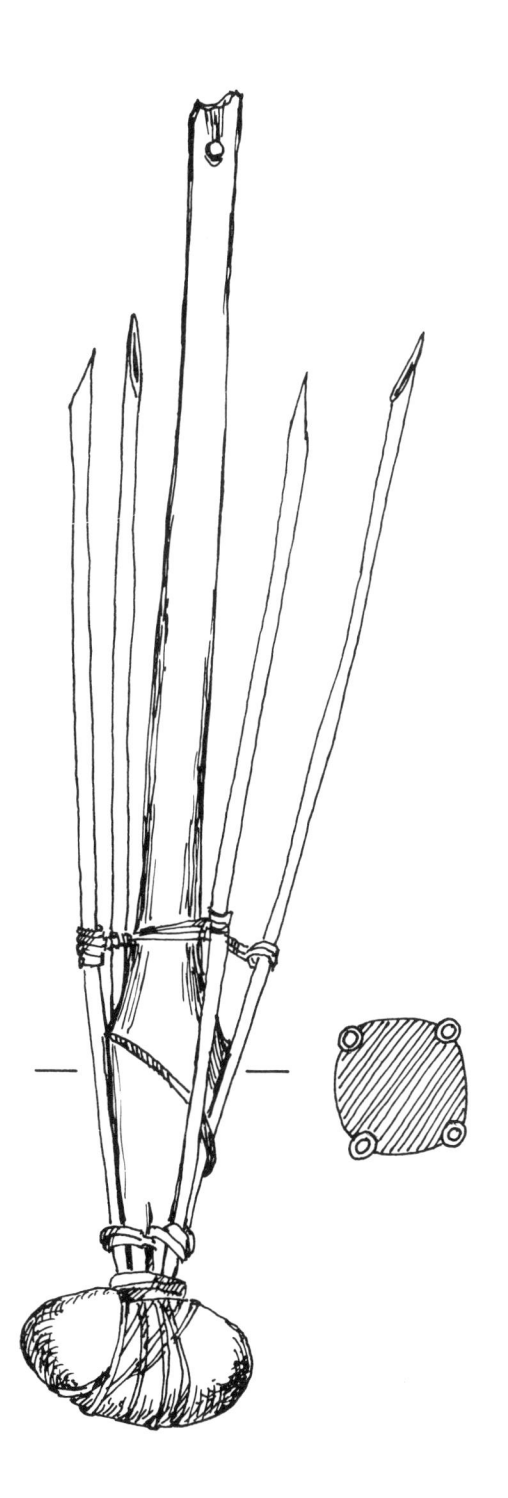

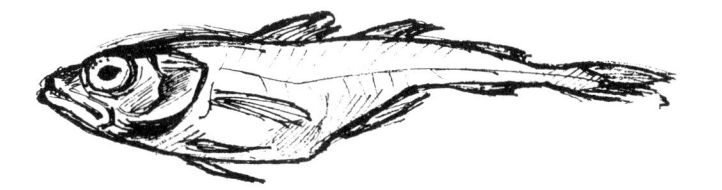

One day during a later visit, we saw a grayfish washed up on the shore down below Qilakitsoq. This is a small arctic type of cod, seldom over 25 cm in length; it is also called polar cod or, in Greenlandic, *eqalugaq*, which means resembling a trout. The grayfish is of great importance as food for the seals, and in olden days it made a welcome change in the daily meat diet for humans. With today's modern fishing methods it is no problem to go after larger fish at great depths, so the grayfish has by now lost its importance and is only occasionally taken.

In the Umanaq district grayfish were caught with a primitive jig, as shown to the left. This is 18 cm long, and its shaft is of wood with four grooves to which four pointed radial wingbones of the northern fulmar have been bound with whale baleen strips. These sharp points function as hooks or barbs. To give weight, a stone in attached, likewise with baleen strips. The barbed implement reproduced alongside was found close to some ancient burials on Umanak Island itself, a full 200 metres over sea level. In similar circumstances bundles of radial wingbones already sharpened as reserve hooks have been found. Only one end of the bones is sharpened, leaving the head of the joint in place, which helps it to be more solidly attached. Without any doubt the Qilakitsoq people used to fish with this sort of multiple barb.

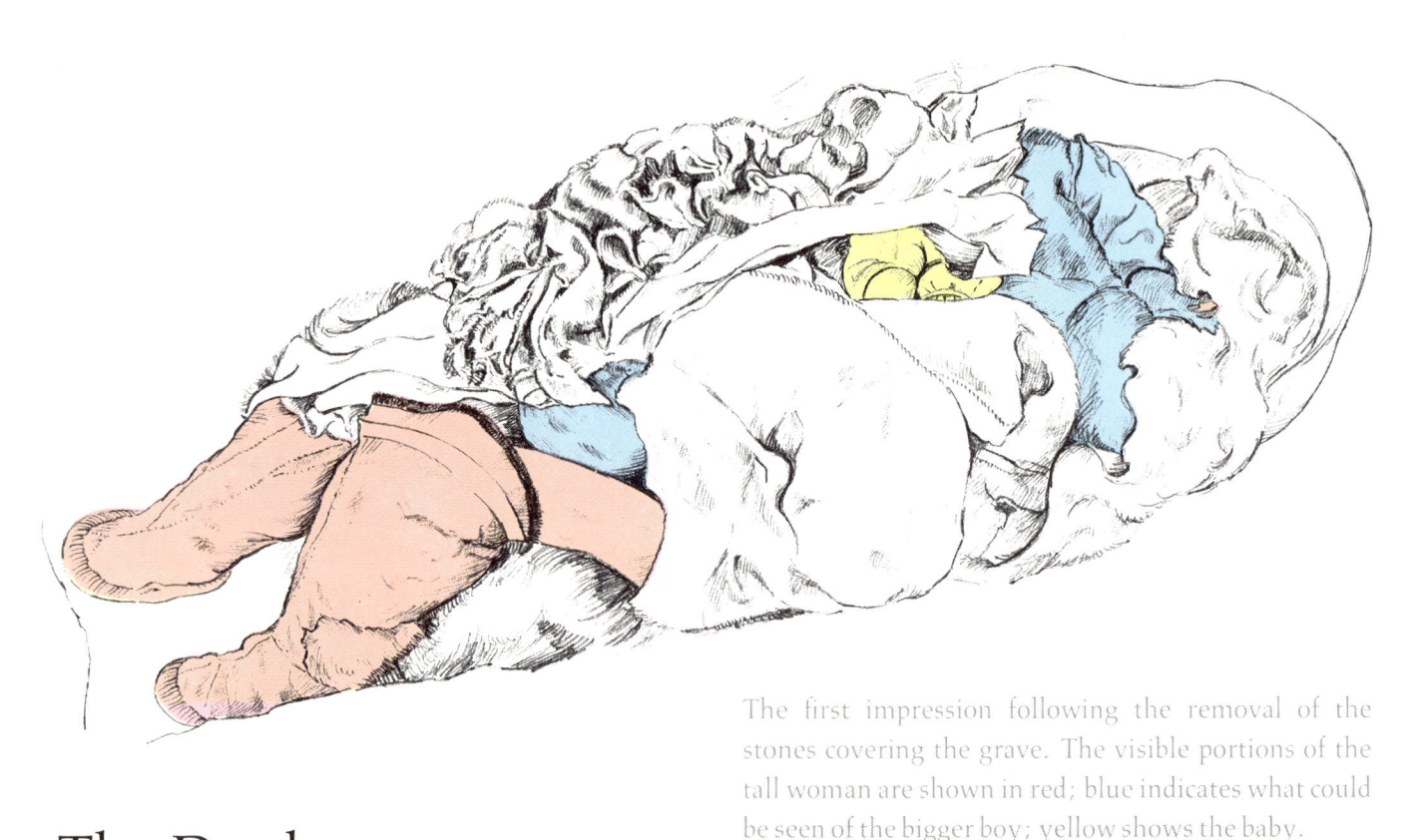

The first impression following the removal of the stones covering the grave. The visible portions of the tall woman are shown in red; blue indicates what could be seen of the bigger boy; yellow shows the baby.

The Dead

FROM OUR FIRST VISIT at Easter 1978 we brought back the two children's desiccated bodies, as already recounted, along with a good many fur items. The bodies were taken to the Institute for Forensic Medicine in Copenhagen, where the first examinations began. At the same time H. Tauber of the National Museum undertook a C-14 test of caribou skin, sealskin and skin from the older child. The dating reached was A.D. 1460 with margin of error of 50 years each way.

As a curious detail, mention can be made that already on collecting the children's bodies we noticed that they were covered with a white layer which resembled a thick cosmetic. This white layer began to spread dangerously in the refrigerating room of the Forensic Medicine Institute. It proved to be a fungus. [NOTE: Laboratory tests showed this to be *sporotrix fungorum*, found in only three other places in the world. NJG] Later it became evident that the best temperature for maintaining the mummies is ordinary room temperature. [NOTE: Eventually gamma radiation removed all traces.]

The second retrieval journey took place in August into September 1978. The members of the expedition this time were my replacement as head

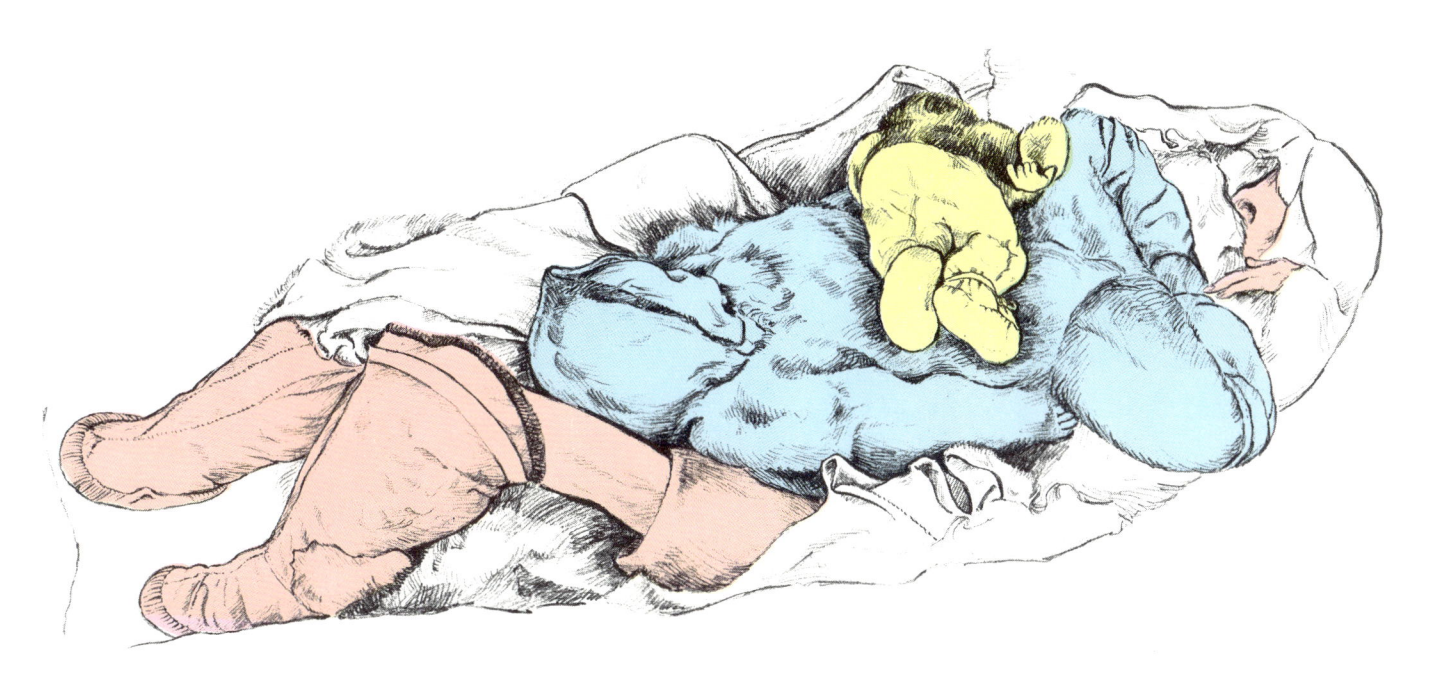

The second view, after removal of the loose furs which lay over the bodies. The big boy is shown in blue, the little one in yellow and the visible portions of the tall woman in red.

of the Greenland Museum, Claus Andersen, the movie maker Jørgen Roos, who filmed the entire progress of the work, and I myself. The remaining six bodies could be removed, and our impressions be affirmed in a combined conclusion:

The first grave we had found contained five bodies. On top, as already mentioned, lay the infant, a boy about half-a-year old, clad in a little fur jacket with anorak hood, and a sort of a 'crawl suit' or leggings and pants in one piece. The fingernails – as the first discoverers had already noted – were remarkably long and claw-like. Corresponding observations both in Greenland and in Denmark had led to the assumption that nails continue to grow for some time after death. In reality the effect is due to the shrinking of the flesh during the process of mummification (in this case desiccation by freeze-drying).

The boy who lay reversed under the baby was a six or seven-year old, at the stage of losing the baby-teeth; the middle front teeth in the upper jaw were missing. His excellently sewed kamiks and fur suit have already been mentioned. [NOTE: subsequent data from Greenland Museum in 1983 placed the age at 4-4½ years old and later muscle tissue type tests show that he could be the son of the tall woman on whose lap he lay.]

The woman under the children was, as stressed earlier, remarkably tall, about 170 cm (5 feet 7 inches). She lay on her back with her legs slightly bent. Her right hand lay over her breast, but pulled up into the sleeve of her fur jacket; her left

The tall woman who lay on top in Grave 1. [NOTE: Later data which the translator of this book obtained in Godthåb in 1983 gave the height of this woman (referred to as 'Number 3') as 65 cm (5 feet 5 inches) and her age as between 20 and 25 years.]

hand in contrast was visible, touchingly beautiful even in its desiccated condition. Her long-tailed sealskin coat could be seen at the armholes to cover an inner garment of bird skins with the black pin-feathers still in place. A pair of short sealskin pants and kamiks of brown scraped sealskin completed the wearing apparel. The pants were so short that the thighs were bare.

The next body ('Number 4'), underneath the tall woman, was a woman who at first glance looked pregnant. Her kamiks, whose toes projected, were coloured Venetian red; they were undoubtedly rubbed with a mixture of blubber and red ochre, which, it happens, can be found on the Nugssuaq peninsula. Under her lay another body, the fifth and last in this grave ('Number 5'). It was wrapped in a great many furs and garments, and one of the furs was bearskin. This body was a woman as well. [NOTE: Information obtained in 1983 put Number 4 at approximately 30 years old, height 145 cm – 4 feet 9 inches. Number 5 is 40-50 years old, her teeth worn down from preparing furs; to judge by her tissue type, she could be the mother of the two younger women above her, in which case three generations of the same family lay here. NJG]

In the neighbouring grave (Grave 2) there were

In Grave 2 on a lower layer of reindeer fur this clump was found. From top to bottom can be seen a 'honey jar' (a disc made of beeswax curved to form a container), a newly-hatched dead honey bee, a cocoon and a clump of bee larvae cells. Life-size.

The so-called 'pregnant' woman ('Number 4').

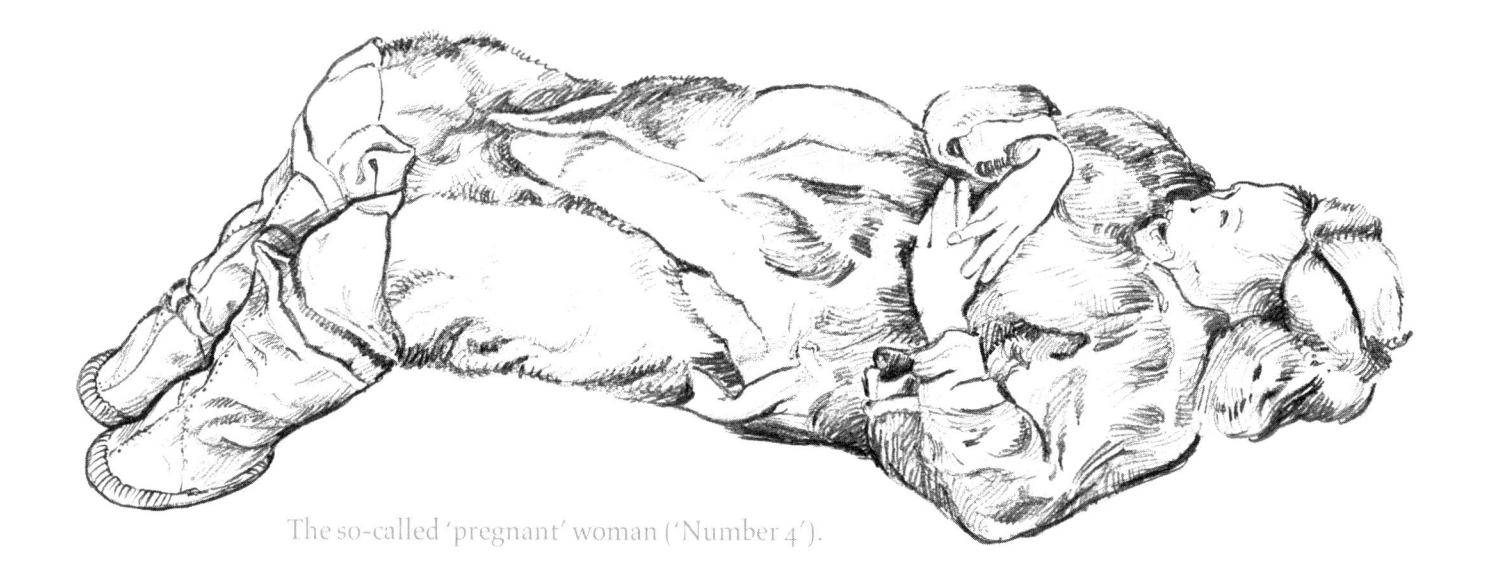

three bodies piled on top of one another, as in the first grave. The top body ('Number 6') lay with the hands withdrawn into the sleeves of the fur garment, and the face completely concealed by the wide anorak hood which was pulled right over it; one end of the fur rug beneath it was pulled up half over the head, as if she slept. The characteristically long boots of an almost violet shade, possibly rubbed with berry juice and blubber, were not well-sewed. The sewing of the soles in particular was rather sloppily done. On the whole, the impression was a bit motley, as the upper part of her pants was made of light red-haired dog fur, while the legs of the pants were of sealskin. [NOTE: Data obtained in Greenland in 1983 put this woman's age at 50-60 years, height *circa* 153 cm or just over 5 feet.]

The woman 'Number 6' rested on a layer of caribou skin and long grass – kamik hay – which was usually gathered near bird-nesting cliffs. On the fur rug below her heels lay three dead bumblebees. Later, during the removal of the bodies, an entire bumblebee's nest fell out, consisting of cocoons, remains of larvae cells and so-called honey jars or wax containers. The woman's left kamik from the heel on to far up the leg was shiny and sticky with honey. To complete the picture as far as insects are concerned, there were dead bluebottle flies and many of their larvae cocoon cases in the upper layers in both graves.

The next body, 'Number 7,' was a young woman whose head was almost separated from her body, hanging by only a few neck sinews. The young woman had strong, healthy teeth, of which a number had fallen out of the jaws. There was some indication that she had had an injury to her left eye, possibly struck by a stray arrow during play in childhood – similar scars from missiles are seen not infrequently among the Eskimos. [NOTE: Data obtained in Greenland in 1983 placed this woman's age at 18-20 years, height *circa* 148 cm. or 4 feet 10½ inches.]

For the third and lowest-lying body, 'Number 8,' the costume was less well-preserved, due to its

The so-called 'pregnant' woman's face ('Number 4'). And how she may have looked when alive. [NOTE: Her age has been placed at *circa* 30 years, height at 145 cm (4 feet 9 inches). Later x-rays showed no sign of a fetus.]

close contact with the ground underneath. [NOTE: Age *circa* 50 years; height *circa* 150 cm or 4 feet 11 inches.] A lesion of earlier date had robbed her of a number of teeth from the upper left jaw. Her lower jaw had fallen off and lay separate on top of the neck. Did the two women maybe receive their lesions in connection with their death?

During the original uncovering of the mummies I was first of the opinion that the bodies in Grave 2 were of men, a conjecture based upon the type of fur hoods. But it later became evident, as more was revealed, that it could not be men; their high hoods had lain so crushed together that it was difficult to identify the cut, and a closer examination of the types of kamik excluded, for the top and for the lowest persons concerned, that they could be men's kamiks – they were too 'impractical' for use on hunting expeditions, and completely impossible to use in kayak travel.

For the middle body, 'Number 7,' in Grave 2 the

The young woman in Grave 2 ('Number 7') wearing the amaut-type fur coat in which to carry her infant. [NOTE: Age: 18-20 years, height 148 cm or 4 feet 10¼ inches. Muscle tissue test showed she could be the daughter of Numbers 5, 6 or 8.]

matter proved more difficult to determine, as the kamiks here were distinctly of a man's type, and the hanging tail on the overgarment was rounded, as in the men's costume. This was the reason in the first round of descriptions that this person was called 'the young man with the fine teeth.' However, on going through some old drawings – to be sure 250 to 300 years younger than these mummies – it became evident that the style of these tailpieces was no certain basis for one's decision.

One day it suddenly became clear to me that this person's hood or cowl had a considerable widening in the neckband – it opened up into a large hood and almost puffed out at the shoulders, hence showed features we know from the *amaut*, a fur coat to carry a child in. Without any doubt this was a young woman, presumably the mother of the little boy. Was the child placed with his grandmother in Grave 1? It would in any case not conflict with Eskimo usage to do this.

Another feature which on the first round had not been grasped was that no one in the 'men's grave' had any indication of beard growth. To be sure, the beard with Inuit men is as a rule more sparse than with Europeans, but in the good state of preservation of these bodies, a beard should be visible.

Accordingly, all the bodies buried here, apart from the two children, were those of women.

On removing the bodies we expected to find

Mother with child in an amaut fur garment with the extended back for carrying the child in. The baby from Qilakitsoq was too little to be able to stick his head out of the opening and so would have lain completely hidden in the coat.

implements and other accessories, a feature well-known in Inuit graves, but we found nothing. On the other hand, we found something else which in an instant brought the dead people so close that we received a deep perception of the world as they conceived it.

When we proceeded to take the second bundle up from Grave 1 ('Number 4') and carefully opened up the covering, we discerned that it was a woman in advanced pregnancy. Her hands rested on top of her stomach exactly as one sees pregnant women do. It was a deeply moving sight. It was as if her hands in death had sensed more emotion than those of a living person.

She was wearing two fur outer garments on top of each other, but the odd thing about her – pregnant as she looked – she still was not wearing the amaut garment with the widened back for carrying the child. It was the usage, actually, that a woman would not be far advanced in her pregnancy before she put on the amaut, partly to show her condition to others in the settlement, partly to 'fool' the malevolent powers into believing that she already had given birth and that any attack on her interior would be pointless – any attack they planned against her offspring would aim for another goal, in this case for the empty amaut. In this way she could carry her child safely on to its birth.

The greater part of the tall hood on her fur jacket had crumbled away, and her long thick hair lay in a pile behind her head. From this and from the hair still in place in front of her head could be discerned that she had had a hairstyle as shown in the drawing on page 31. In the section of the fur robe around her hips a hole had been worn, and out of this fell a few fragments of leather as the corpse was lifted under considerable difficulty from the grave.

When I took these small bits into my hands they looked at first merely like tufts of fur, but before I had a chance to look at them more closely, the wind had blown the fur away, and in the palm of my hand remained two small bits of leather, two tiny kamik soles, dangling by a sinew thread from a small piece of caribou hide. I am acquainted personally with the meaning of such kamik soles in an indirect way, namely through a sacrificial ritual which has been practised throughout Greenland from Thule to Angmagssalik down to our present century.

After a bear has been killed and brought back to the settlement, the following procedure begins: the flayed pelt with the head still on it is brought into the house. Above the bear's head a piece of meat is hung along with a pair of cut-out kamik soles, and, if the bear is a male, a hunting implement, harpoon or lance; if it is a female, a woman's implement, an ulo (special knife for women's use) or a sewing kit. These things are gifts to the dead animal's spirit. The bear is a great wanderer, therefore the soles of its paws must be strong.

An Inuit's existence is like the bear's. It is a sort of long Arctic expedition, which requires strong shoe soles and warm kamiks. Nothing is warmer than caribou fur, that is why it is a bit of this material the amulet soles have been hung from. The woman to whose coat an amulet of this kind has been attached is a 'simple' amulet-wearer in that the amulet's magic power is to work only on her children and not upon her own self. It is first and foremost the sons who are considered, as they

The Greenland woman's traditional hairstyle is the topknot. It can be claimed with certainty that the Qilakitsoq women's hairdo of five hundred years ago was as shown in this drawing. It is a portrait of the young woman Aiainark from Thule, a free rendering of Count Harald Moltke's drawing in his book *Grønland*. Moltke accompanied the Danish literary expedition to Greenland in 1902-1904.

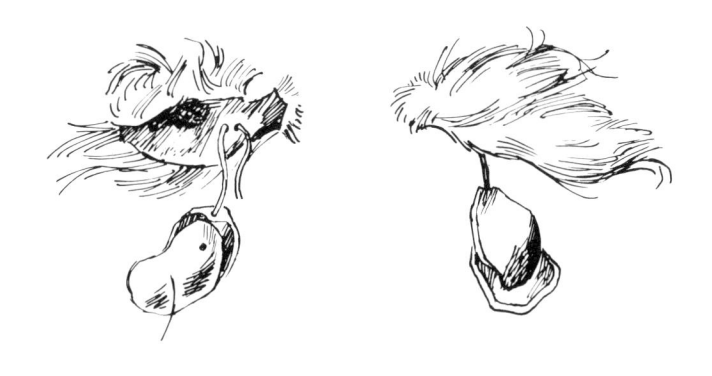

The sole amulet seen from both sides.

will some day, protected by good warm foot gear, through the results of their hunting lead her into a comfortable old age. For her daughters the effect of the amulet's magic power shall be carried on through them to their coming sons.

The sole amulet was given an extra dimension of interpretation later, in the conservation department of the National Museum. A rust-coloured granular spot on the inner or 'meat' side of the bit of caribou skin proved, when Conservator Gerda Møller placed it under the microscope, indeed to be rust, and an x-ray picture taken later revealed that a small piece of iron, undoubtedly a broken sewing needle, was fastened to the leather. So not only warm kamiks, but also well-sewed watertight ones! It will be exciting to obtain the analysis of the iron. Is it from the famous meteoric ironstones whose district lies 750 kilometres further northward, or had it been obtained from the Norsemen whose nearest settlements lay 750 kilometres to the south? There is, however, the third possibility, that the iron comes from Disko or the Umanaq district itself. From around the beginning of the Christian era, the Inuit in Greenland seem to have acquired an ever-increasing taste for iron, and to have been constantly on the lookout for it. They may have had an 'iron mine' which we do not know of today. Tradition tells of people from Disko Bay and the Nugssuaq area who at the big meeting and market-place Taseralik at the mouth of Nordre Strømfjord offered iron for sale that was found in their district. A small bit of

The baby is about a half-year old and measures 43 centimetres [17 inches]. On its breast can be seen the small folded bit of leather. [NOTE: No muscle tissue test was made on the baby to determine which of the young women it could have belonged to. One would assume the one on whose breast it lay face down.]

The view from the grave site, looking northward. The closest points in the landscape are Umanaq Island and Big Island, or Sagdliaruseq.

iron, enough for the tip of a harpoon point, could fetch in payment a paddle oar to use on the whale hunt, fashioned of the choicest piece of driftwood, and carefully edged with bone.

But there were more amulets in the grave. On the breast of the smaller child's fur jacket was a small piece of leather, scraped bare of fur and folded over. Even though the piece of leather apparently contains nothing, there can be no doubt but that it is a soot-amulet – the inner side of the leather must have been rubbed with soot. The idea was that soot outlasts fire and therefore must be stronger. This strength is passed on to the wearer of it, who will become strong and invulnerable to armed attack and to sorcery.

What can be assumed to be a third amulet is visible so far as a black foreign object in the bottom pleat in what seems to be the tail of a woman's outer garment. My guess is that it is the forehead skin of a black guillemot. If this holds true, we are looking at a rare amulet. It is not often that women wear amulets; they are exposed to less danger than men, who go out onto ice and sea on their hunts and therefore have far greater need of protection than the women in the settlement and camping-ground. This is a birth-amulet, an amulet to make giving birth easier for the wearer. As birth-amulets the forehead skin of the three-toed seagull is known; this little gull lays eggs small in comparison to its size, so the amulet wearer will therefore bear children with small heads. The black guillemot does not lay such small eggs, so one cannot directly compare the two birds, but the guillemot has a narrow head, and it is specially speedy in gliding out from its nesting-place on the cliff, a feature which passes on to the woman who wears the bird's forehead feathers as an amulet, and it will take effect on the day she bears her child.

[The black guillemot shown on page 5.]

Qilakitsoq around A.D. 1460, seen from the northeast. The first snow has fallen, the sea level is low, and in the small bay below the settlement, the water is thick with ice slush.

In the foreground are the two dwellings. The kayaks and the umiak (woman boat) have been set up on stands; the space under the umiak houses various supplies and in general serves as a storage shed.

In front of each entrance passage a stick has been placed in the snow; this is the 'snow knocker' – because no Inuk goes indoors before he has knocked all the snow off his clothing. The dark patch out from each entrance passage is the garbage pile.

Near the houses can be seen the settlement's few dogs – they could not afford in those days to keep and feed large dog-teams.

From the settlement can be seen a path that goes away up to a large prominent rock, the settlement's lookout. From up here there is a wide view out across the water, and from there people have always been able to follow the migration of the sea mammals and other passing traffic. For a settlement this is of vital importance, so there is almost always someone on the lookout there. The hunters out on the fjord always kept an eye on the lookout post, because the women could summon them home by lighting a smoky bonfire. The path can still be distinctly seen today in the vegetation, after 500 years, and the black lichen has been worn away along it up the hillside.

Beneath the large bulge of the cliff to the right of the lookout was the burial site. Other graves lay parallel with the cliffs and up against the precipices, some of them hundreds of metres up the mountainside.

Along the bay and out towards the lowest rock shelf to the south are traces of many buildings, and everywhere refuse from Stone Age man's working of tools.

According to tradition Qilakitsoq was in olden days one of the best and most sought-after wintering places in the Umanaq district, so there may well have been twenty or so people here in the dark period of the year.

The overhang under which the graves were found must have been formed in earlier times, when the lower part of the rock bulge detached itself and slid downwards. At the base of the hollow thus formed was a sharp-angled crevice, which the burial party made use of. The space was narrow, so the bodies had to be piled one over the other. Standing at the two crevices, one gets the impression that the dead people's legs were first pushed down, after which their shoulders were pulled down in. Especially the two lowest women in Grave 1 were well shoved down; we had to prod and pull at them before the proper angle was found so that we could pull them out.

Over the open tops of the two graves flat covering stones were laid, some of which can be reckoned to weigh up to fifty kilos, and on top of them a layer of fragments was carefully laid to conceal all traces.

There can be no doubt that the dead were all buried on the same day, but mass burials are indeed rare occurrences. What can have happened to these people? Victims of a sickness? Doubtful. Starved to death? Not that either, they look too well-nourished for that. The most likely thing is that 500 years ago they came travelling along in their umiak, to settle for the winter in Qilakitsoq, just below the place where their bodies have so recently been found. A huge stranded iceberg may have lost an upended layer of its ice as they moved past, so that the entire party perished in a welter of ice in the violent waves. Especially to protect the settlement from flood-waves of calving icebergs, it had been placed far back on the level terrain, 30 to 40 metres distance from the shore and a dozen metres above sea level.

The skerries outside of Qilakitsoq bay, looking westward at low tide, on an evening at the beginning of September.

The men in their kayaks who had accompanied or followed the women's umiak escaped, salvaged the dead and carried them a good fifty metres up the mountainside to bury them carefully under the projecting rock, where no rain or snow falls and the sun touches the grave site only for a very short time at midsummer. For 500 years they were preserved thanks to the constant dryness and shade.

The careful placing of the bodies may also be interpreted as a desire that the settlement's women and children who had died would have a good place with the most beautiful view to be found. And not only that: they should be well protected from the rough weather.

So now we can understand why no men's tools were found in the graves, because when everything that had drifted ashore after the wreck was collected together, the women were given their clothing and fur coverings in their graves, while the men kept what remained of their own clothing, which had also been carried in the big umiak; they would sorely need everything for the coming winter, without their women to prepare skins, and sew, and make their clothes.

I have no words to describe the extent of the catastrophe and the anguish it must have brought with it. And if the reader of these lines puts aside the book for a moment and pictures to himself or herself that the women connected closely with one's own life, all perished at one and the same time – all of them – and possibly all the younger children with them – one can understand what the situation was for the men of Qilakitsoq. The thought is a hard one to harbour in our mind.

The eight persons stricken by that disaster may well have been half of all the people who had decided, that fall of presumably about the middle of the 1400s, to spend the winter at the Qilakitsoq settlement. The Umanaq district at that point in time was anything but densely populated. The vast fjord-complex with a fishing and hunting area

Icebergs, seen towards northwest from the shore at Qilakitsoq.

of not less than 14,000 square kilometres would scarcely be inhabited by more than 100 to 200 individuals spread through 15 to 20 settlements. The disaster therefore claimed an appreciable part of the total population, an event that would cause a great hue and cry but that eventually was forgotten. It is difficult to connect this particular event with any traditions about burials that took place in this neighbourhood. Some local people think that the burial was discovered 100 years ago and then forgotten again; and that it was seen on another occasion 50 years ago. On both those occasions it would likely be a mere peek into the grave, as the time when Hans Grønvold first saw it. But those two discoveries would have taken place at a time when there was still the greatest respect paid to heathen graves and to the sorcery connected to them. There is information extant about finds of mummified bodies for all parts of Greenland, and in the course of time many of these will be able to be followed up.

The discovery at Qilakitsoq gives us a well-founded hope for still other well-preserved finds. It is first and foremost in the history of costume that they will be able to lead us even further back in time.

The Eskimos' Clothing

THE PRINCIPLE IN THE CONSTRUCTION or design of the eskimo costume cannot be better illustrated than through the legend of the Moon Man, a ferocious personage who from his home up on the moon kept watch to be sure that people in the settlements on earth carried out the rules for exacting the death penalty. The Moon Man also ruled over both ebb and flood tide, and had power over the fertility of humans and animals, birds and fish. Often the local exorcist had to undertake a dangerous journey in order to persuade the Moon Man to make a childless woman fertile.

If a human being transgressed the rules governing the death penalty, the Moon Man came sailing in, clad as a bear from top to toe, to strike the bold transgressor and his dwelling-place with his rod, a prodigious-sized narwhal tusk. His anorak (i.e. hooded outer garment) was an entire bearskin which had been peeled inside out in one piece off the slain animal after its back legs were scored along the thighbone and the forepaws were detached around the wrist. The opening around the gaping jowls became the hole in the hood through which the Moon Man's face projected. The fur of the forepaws became mitts, and from the hide of the legs, trousers and kamiks were made. In both the front and the back of the jacket a 'tail' or tip hung down – the bear's genitals and tail – and it is especially these 'tails' that we find in such prominence on eskimo fur jackets.

When a woman sews a fur coat she is in reality reconstructing a male animal. The fur coat becomes in its essential appearance and individuality like that of the Moon Man. An animal's fur has been peeled off inside out. The opening for the face is the open jowls of the creature, the arms are its forelegs; sex organs and tail are not forgotten. The sex-indicating tip on a fur is called *kineq*, i.e. 'to hold out' in the same sense as to extend on nature's behalf; a different way for saying the sex organ. The back tail drop is called *akoq*, i.e. the behind part.

It is not enough that the animal's fur coat is recreated – the bones are marked on the surface in the form of inset light or dark stripes, for instance, on the outer side of the sleeve; on the tall hoods worn by women the ornament goes across the entire central line front to back. This 'nose bridge' type of ornamentation can, however, best be recognized in the man's hood, where it runs from the front edge of the hat up to the crown. This decoration corresponds to the bridge of the nose of the bear or of any other animal. On the hood is often found a triangular stripe that extends from the shoulder and part way up the side of the hood. The carefully and clearly defined edgings along all the coat's openings are precise markings of those joints to which the knife has been put, in order to

The idea in the design of the Eskimo costume.

roll the skin off the animal. The captured and slain animals' souls were supposed to be pleased by this tribute to them, and if the correct method was used, an animal would return to let itself be caught anew. This concept also is the basis for the reconstruction of the animal's 'covering' when it is to be sewn into clothing after proper preparation. By causing the animal's coat to be resurrected unchanged, it is shown the respect its spirit demands – and the human being, in return, receives the animal's ability to survive the rigours of nature.

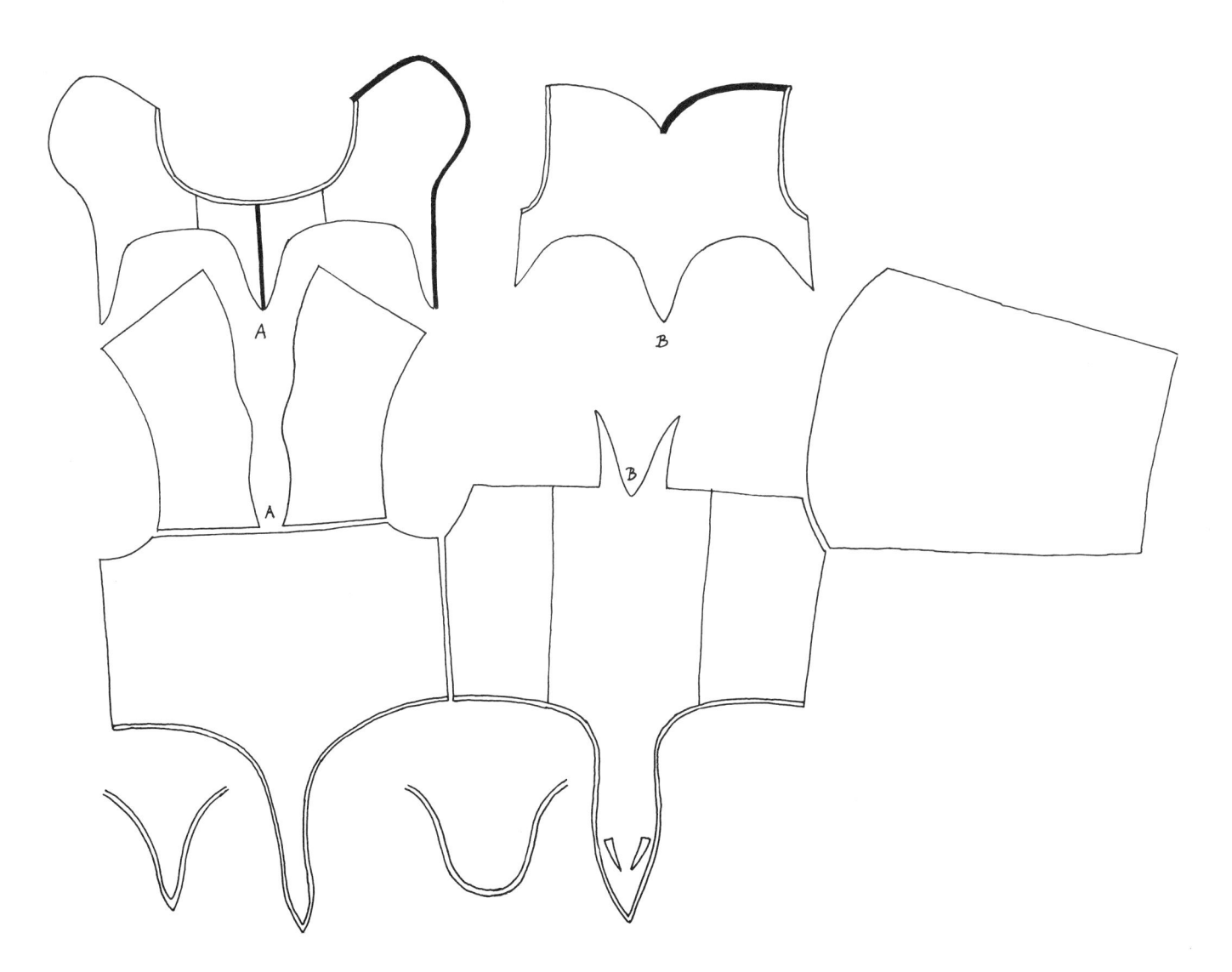

At the present time of writing [NOTE: for book published in 1979] it is not possible to obtain a clear impression in detail of 'our' Thule Eskimo bodies' costume design. For one thing, the costumes are stiff and have to be treated and straightened out; another thing is that the fur hairs on them vary partially in colour, or are discoloured due to the afore-mentioned fungus, and change of colour from brown to yellow makes the total effect all too variegated or motley. But in spite of that, a couple of well-preserved outer jackets for women which lay loose have provided such clear design details that is can be stated with certainty that the same design is found unchanged in a Thule woman's coat from 1909. It is the newer costume which was the basis for the drawings of the pattern as shown on page 40. The only difference is that the newer fur coat has considerably shorter tailpieces than the old.

It has been more difficult to work out the pattern of the men's costume, but in the main features the cut seems very alike for both sexes. A sketch reconstructing a woman and a man in costume shows better than any words can, how similar or how different they were when they wore their clothes (pages 44-45).

When we look at the Qilakitsoq people's costume we must ask ourselves how long such tailpieces have been in style. The long tailpieces on the women's costume were loose-hanging, flapping affairs, and the costume cannot have been particularly comfortable to walk in. But as already indicated, there was strong motivation for their preservation. The tailpieces constantly accompany Inuit people, most markedly in northern Canada. In Greenland they have steadily grown less large in the course of the past 150 to 100 years; they are now so small that their kinsmen in Canada call the Greenlanders *Akukitormiut* – the people of small tailpieces.

In the Thule district the tailpieces are still found on the woman's *amaut* – the anorak she carries her child in, and in the costume both men and women wear for travelling. On the entire west coast of Greenland the tailpieces are retained in caribou-skin coats, where the caribou tail is kept on for both front and back sections; on the anorak hood the ears of the animal are often retained.

Pattern of a woman's outer jacket. This is the regular jacket, not the one a mother uses for carrying her child in. In the main features there seems not to be any difference between the woman's or the man's outer jacket; the former appears somewhat wider, and the sleeves are long in comparison. The woman's hood is high but of such small depth at the back that her face was completely bared when the hood was in place over her head. The men's hoods are cut to project sharply at the front edge and protect the face effectively.

The front and back tailpiece for women was 40 to 45 cm in length. The two inset diagonal designs can be interpreted as eyes, the watchful spirit of the tailpiece keeping its eyes on whatever approached from the rear.

The man's tailpiece for front and for back is shown in same relative proportion. Note that the woman's hood (to left) is basically sewed together along the back of the head and up over the crown to the forehead, while the man's is sewed together in front of the chin and at the top. In both women's and men's a dark stripe is inserted, the so-called nose bridge ornament. For women it seems that as a status mark, the narrower and darker the stripe is, the finer, hence the stripe is most frequently cut from the black patch on the back of the Greenland seal, while for men the decorative nose bridge stripe seems to be made of the darkest part along the back of the ring seal; it is wider than the women's, sometimes a combination of three stripes, with the dark middle stripe flanked by two white stripes – the leg fur of a white dog.

The reconstruction drawings on this and the following pages are an attempt to give an impression of how the Thule Eskimos in the 1400s were clothed at Qilakitsoq and likely along the whole coast of West Greenland. The sketches are made on the basis of the costumes found in the graves, and in a manner so as to be recognized directly from the main text of this volume. All the sketches show newly-sewed costumes that exhibit no signs of wear, as we can imagine they were when the dead bodies were buried back in the 1400s.

It is quite conceivable that these women of Qilakitsoq and their parents witnessed Norsemen on hunting trips in what the latter called the 'Northern range' – in any case their grandparents would have seen them at the end of the 1300s.

The uppermost woman in Grave 2. Her pants are of dogskin at the top, lengthened below with sealskin. Her kamiks are simple in every way, but brand new. At the time of removal from the site the tops of the kamiks looked bluish purple in colour, but later changed to grey-black. [NOTE: This woman, given the number 'Six', was 153 cm tall (5 feet ¼ inch) and judged to be between 50 and 60 years of age.]

The lowest figure in Grave 2, a woman with a lesion in the upper jaw. Her jacket sleeves seem somewhat shorter than those of all the other women. [NOTE: She is 'Number Eight', 150 cm (4 feet 11 inches) tall and about 50 years of age.]

This free reconstruction shows a woman with a small child on her arm; she is clad in an eiderduck shirt, with the feathers turned inward.

43

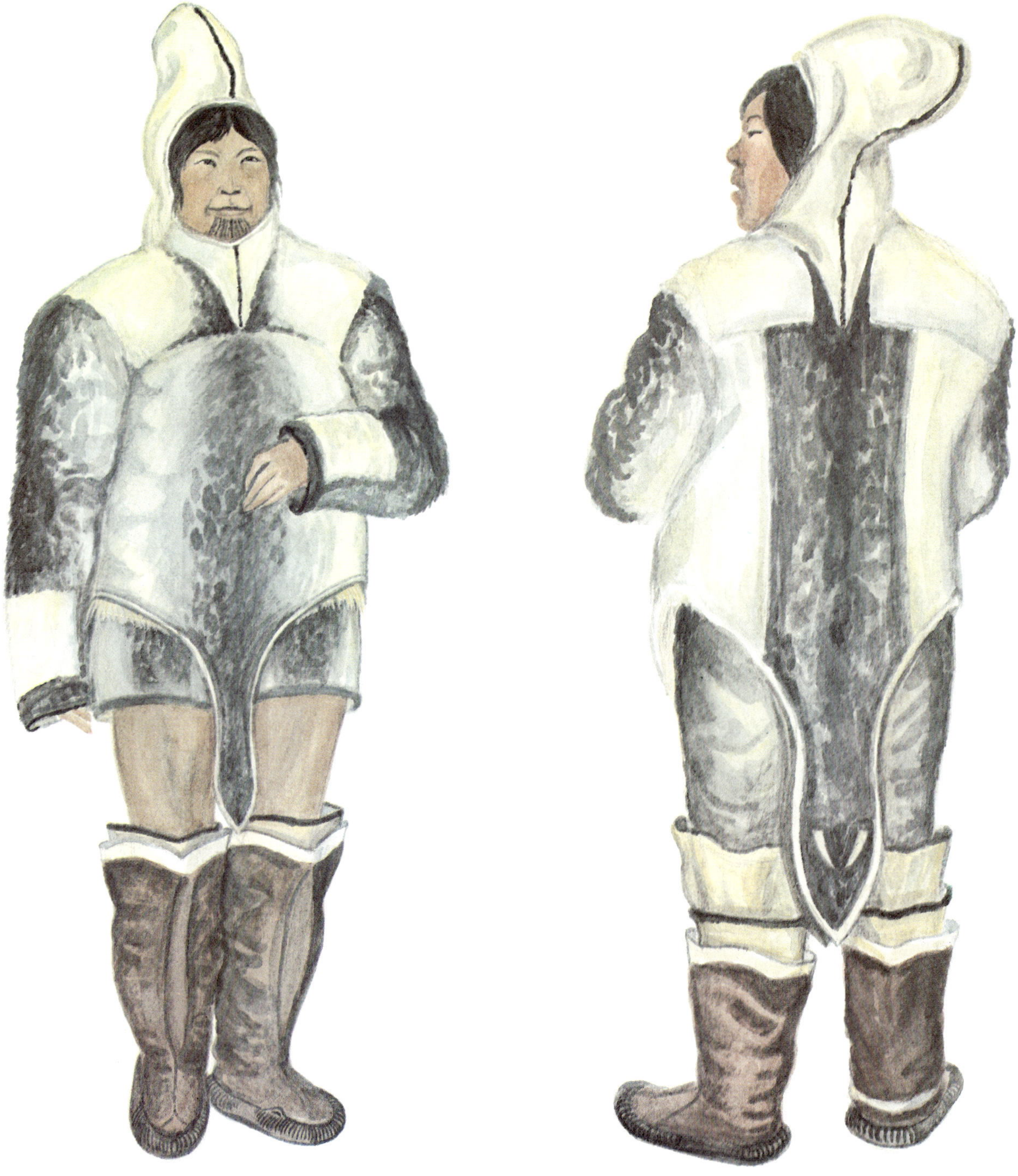

The tall 170 cm [5 feet 7 inches] woman, 'Number Three' of the bodies. Note the caribou fur projecting from under the outer fur jacket at the hips, also the two white inlaid ornamental pieces on the sleeves – these are known from water colours which the English artist John White made in 1577 from some eskimos brought back from northern Canada to England by the Frobisher expedition. This is the first time we have proof of these same decorative patch-insets in Greenland.

The woman in the centre here was inspired by the one lying second from the top in Grave 1, who at first sight seemed to be pregnant, but to judge on the basis of the clothes she wore could scarcely have been so. Her kamiks at the time of removal from the site had a reddish colour, but later became darker brown. A band of the light belly skin of a seal encircles her right ankle. Note the three back panels, the central one of choice dark fur, flanked by light belly skin, also carefully selected. The tailpiece spirit's eyes guard the wearer against rear attack. Note how little depth there is to the back of the hood – the woman's face is entirely exposed. This costume was basically reconstructed from a woman's fur coat lying among the furs wrapped around the bodies.

As the dead adults were all women, this man's outfit, with the rounded tailpiece and the wide 'nose bridge' ornament in three stripes on the hood, was sketched on the basis of the two boys' outfits. With the Inuit, the children's suits are true copies of grown men's.

45

The 4½ year-old boy. His kamiks provided the model for those of the man in the preceding picture – they are in every respect more carefully worked than those of the women.

About 1940 a very distinctive little sculpture carved in walrus tusk was found in Thule. Its exact age cannot be determined, but it may well be up to 3000 years old. The sculpture shows two birds together back to back; the birds are little auks (Danish søkonge) and they look fetus-like. They are both pointed at the lower end. In the one an oval hole is hollowed out – unmistakably a female. The other ends at the bottom in the head of a dog – the old eskimo expression for the male organ. Because the sexes, as we have seen, are symbolized in the front tailpiece, we can claim with confidence that the carver wore a costume with tailpieces. The tailpiece tradition is in all probability at least as old as the Inuit culture, which today can be followed back in time for 5000 years.

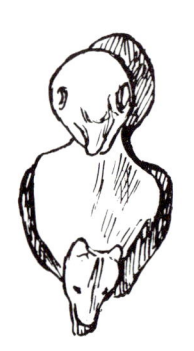

The animals shown on this page were an important basis of existence for the Inuit.

Polar bear.

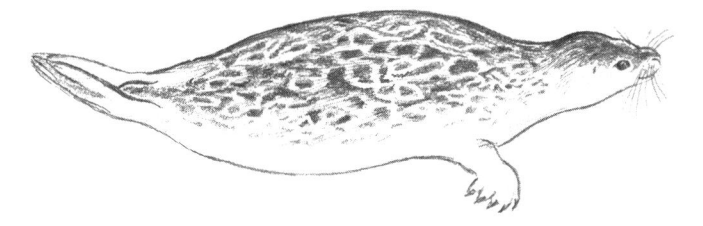

Caribou.

The ring seal, most important of all the species of seal, among other reasons because its skin was an essential part of the eskimo costume.

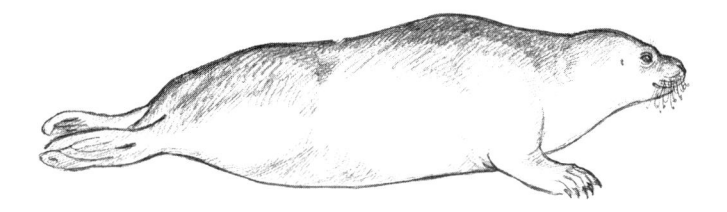

Young Greenland seal, also called blue-side.

The thong seal, whose hide is especially used for shoe soles and dog sled traces.

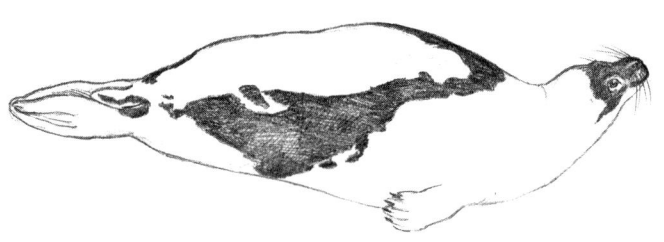

The full-grown Greenland seal, or black-side.

If we look at old hunting cultures in Europe we find at Cogul in Spain a rock painting called 'The Women's Dance.' Is that not tailpiece costumes they are dancing in?

Women's dance. Detail of a rock painting from Cogul in Spain, here taken from *The First Human Beings*.

Once upon a time those ice age hunters roamed the land, a people that in their religion and magic had to pay heed to the same conditions and rules for good luck in hunting as did the Inuit. All available means were employed to appease the sensitive spirits of the animals they hunted – even the costume's appearance was of importance. It would be strange if the tailpiece garb had not been swung around here in our own country of Denmark ten thousand years ago.

Of ornamentation in the mummies' costume that of the nose bridge has been proved with certainty, both in the women's dress and in that of the two boys. A dark triangle on a hood that is unfortunately very weatherbeaten may be the remnant of a shape indicating an ear. As it happens, the hoods on the fur jackets the dead lay in were in generally poor state of preservation. In the case of the tall woman and the young one with the fine teeth, the head was uncovered, while the others had their hood pulled down over their head. The Qilakitsoq people's costumes, as far as could be confirmed, were sparingly decorated, yet these sparse ornaments show the 'skeleton ornamentation' which we know today specially in the East Greenlanders' grotesque *tulipak* figures. The skeleton ornamentation can be followed back for 3000 years in Greenland, and has reached its most colourful development in the present-day women's festive costume in East and West Greenland.

If one tries to describe the thought process behind the Eskimos' costume, this coincides on such a close tangent with the concept of the amulet usage that is is not exaggerated to call the costume as a whole the most visible or largest amulet in use, namely a protective amulet which gives the so weak and naked creature – the human being – immense freedom of movement. Clad in his costume, mankind has taken on himself the characteristics of animals and achieved the ability to move, warm and confident, through cold and storm.

The skeleton as ornamentation leads us into another cult concept, that of spirit worship. Within the limbs of all living beings resides a tiny spirit in the exact image of its bearer. When the spirit is present, each limb becomes an individual that thinks for itself – the limbs can be moved independently of one another, and this flexibility, to be sure in simplified form, is transferred to the costume by means of the skeleton ornamentations.

The Qilakitsoq people's costumes were unusually beautifully sewed; the stitches are placed precisely close together and smoothed down with the greatest care. In the present condition of the furs [NOTE: as of the time of the publication of the 1979 book, a year after the find was removed to Denmark] they are stiff and wrinkled, hence need to be fingered and looked at carefully to recognize where the stitches are. [NOTE: Just under eighty articles of clothing, including the garments worn by the eight people and several articles lying loose, as well as many uncut animal skins in which they were wrapped or placed between, were recorded at the National Museum. Listed on page 149 of the 'big' Quilakitsoq book, 1985, they include:

16 sealskin outer coats
1 of reindeer skin
9 inner coats of birdskin
12 pairs of pants (11 outer, 1 inner)
19 high boots (kamiks)
21 stockings
1 pair of half-sleeves]

The eskimo fur coat can be worn inside out, the rule being that in cold weather the fur side faces out – it is then warmer – and in warm weather the leather inner side faces out, which makes the coat less warm to wear. This explains the fine sewing; no one is to criticize an Inuit woman's stitching. This extreme skill in sewing could be 'attained' by women, at least in part, by them having themselves tattooed by means of a soot-blackened thread drawn under the skin's surface – an adorn-

The king eiderduck. Above, male, below, female.

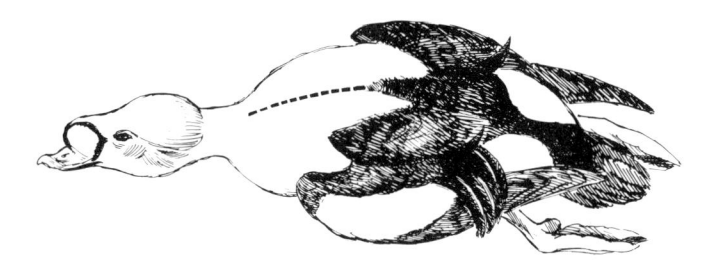

This and the following drawings will show how the eiderduck skin is prepared for use in a shirt. First, the killed bird is scored along the back.

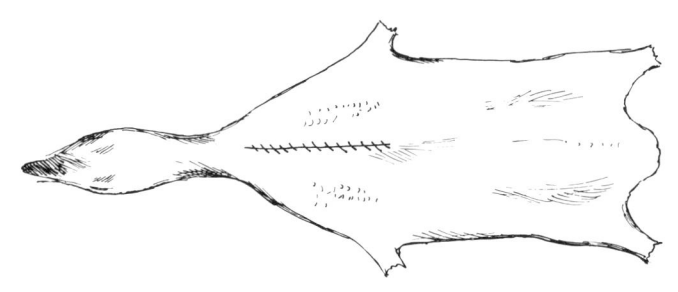

Before the fat is scraped off, the skin is turned inside out, and the cut opening on the back is often stitched together again to protect the feathers from being soiled by grease.

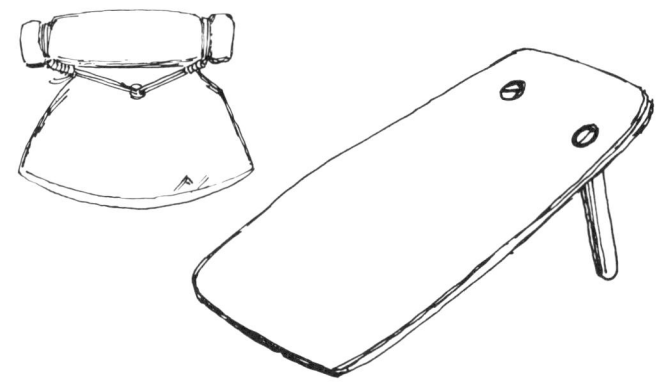

The wings and claws are removed, the stiff shoulder feathers are removed and the feather skin is rolled off the bird's body.

The scraping takes place in two stages. First the birdskin is laid on the scraping board and the main fat is removed with an ulo (woman's knife). In order to extract further fat from the skin, this is then scraped with a large blue mussel shell, which is used almost like a spoon with which the fat is scooped away. After this the scraping board cannot be used any more, as the wood is now totally impregnated with fat which could smudge the cleaned skin.

After thorough, hard scraping the skin is hung up to dry, as a rule inside the house or tent. After this drying, the skin is laid aside for a while.

The eiderduck's skin is folded together along the back and breastbone line, and left lying like this for one night.

When it seems to be time, the dry stiff skin is taken out, and by gumming between the teeth (not chewing), the last remnants of fat are driven out and the skin now remains soft. This takes a great many 'small bites'.

The skin is afterwards thoroughly washed in the urine tub in order to remove any remaining vestiges of grease. The moisture is pressed out with a clam shell.

tailored and sewed they are softened once more, this time with pumice-stone which comes from Icelandic volcanoes and has drifted to Greenland with the ocean current. There are pumice-stone deposits near Godtháb, and the porous and gritty mineral is traded and sold far and wide.

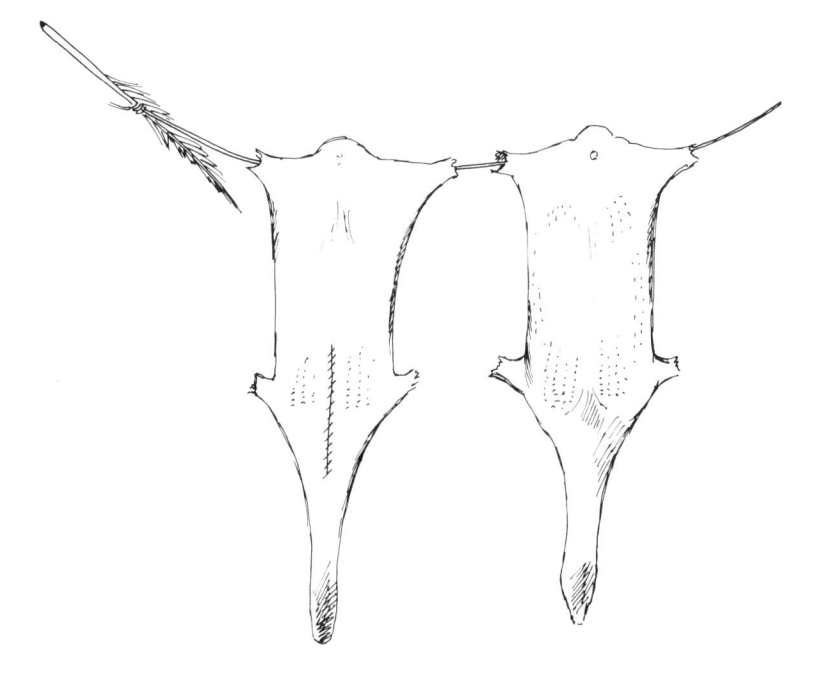

The birdskin is stretched out on a narrow thong to whose one end the flight feather of a seagull is attached; the flight feather serves as a needle, and the thong is pulled through the leg openings. The skins are then hung outdoors in freezing temperatures, and dry in a few days.

When the birdskin has been cut open it is again hung out in the severe cold, from which its inner skinside (literally 'meatside') takes on a fine creamy colour, and the feathers become entirely dry. This process is called 'cold tanning', plain and simple. Before the skins are

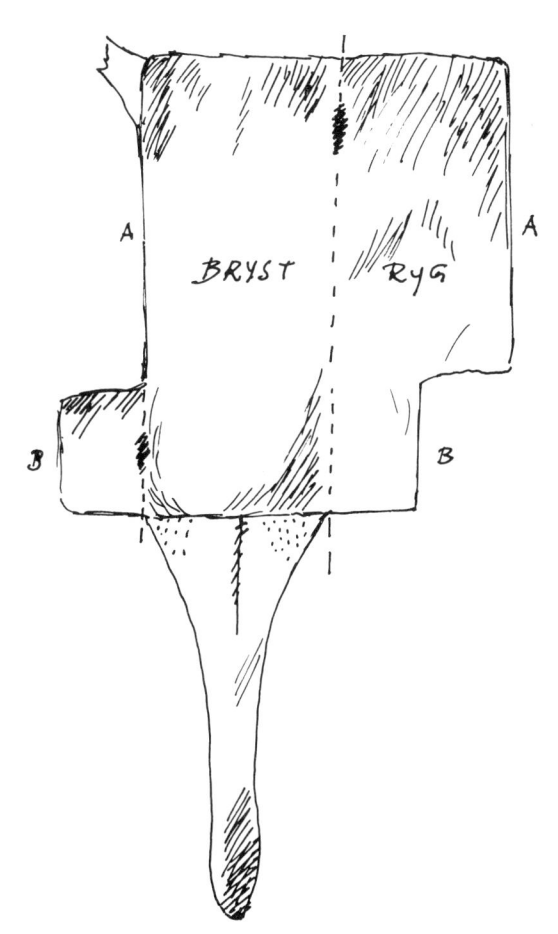

When the birdskin is opened up, this pattern – basically schematized – is shown. The neck and head skin with the beautiful colours in both the ordinary and the king eiderduck are best used for small containers and bags.

ment it is hoped the discovered women's bodies will reveal (see illustrations pages 24-29). It is no empty talk that, as the saying goes, 'A clever sewing-woman makes her husband into a good hunter.' And one ancient poet boasted of his wife's sewing ability as follows:

> The woman at my side
> Has fingertips as small as any spider's,
> Those stitches that she makes
> You have to look for carefully, to see.

For sewing-thread, plaited sinew threads and the skin of a seal's gullet (oesophagus) were used. The Inuit today prefer the gullet skin of the 'black-sided' seal (mature Greenland seal), and we will scarcely be wrong in assuming that the Qilakitsoq folk preferred this seal's long tough gullet skin for making soles. This skin has the characteristic of swelling when wet, and thereby fills out the stitch-holes and renders them watertight.

In both graves there were scraps of eiderduck skin, as well as whole prepared skins. Both male and female high arctic king eiderduck could be identified, and even if this bird does not nest in the Umanaq district it is still the most common species in the area. Modern banding of birds has shown that the entire population of Canada's and West Greenland's male eiderducks and young birds migrates to central West Greenland in order to moult their flight feathers, and Umanaq belongs to this moulting area. It was the tradition since time immemorial in districts from the South District of Egedesminde up to a little north of Upernavik to conduct drives upon the resting, flightless birds in August and on into early September. People gathered at definite localities where from their kayaks and umiaks they drove the swimming birds on to the shore, where they were clubbed to death. In the Egedesminde district in particular, a single drive could see hundreds of birds killed. In our day this form of hunt is no longer allowed.

I cannot conceive of any other method of hunting eiderduck in those early days which would provide enough skins for inner shirts for everyone. A couple of the dead women in the grave were wearing an inside coat made of the breast skin of eiderduck, from which the pin-feathers had not been plucked out. This observation was made from skins projecting below the outer jackets. The eiderduck garments were exact copies of the sealskin coats in design, and in favourable weather conditions they were worn as the sole garment, including out of doors.

Of other clothing, two pairs of women's short house pants were found in the graves. Like the other leather articles they are very dried out and crushed; the one pair has lost so much of its fur that one can only guess that it is sewed of caribou leather. On the other hand the second pair – almost truss- or bikini-like – can be definitely determined. It is sewed of the head- and leg-skin of caribou, and the quality or the thickness of the fur establishes that the caribou was killed at the end of July or beginning of August. A detail in the colour patterning in the leg-skins shows that the caribou's front leg-skin was cut along the front side of the leg, while the skin strips taken from the deer's back leg show that those skins had been cut from the back angle of the back leg – exactly as the hunters of wild caribou or reindeer in Greenland today flay their catch.

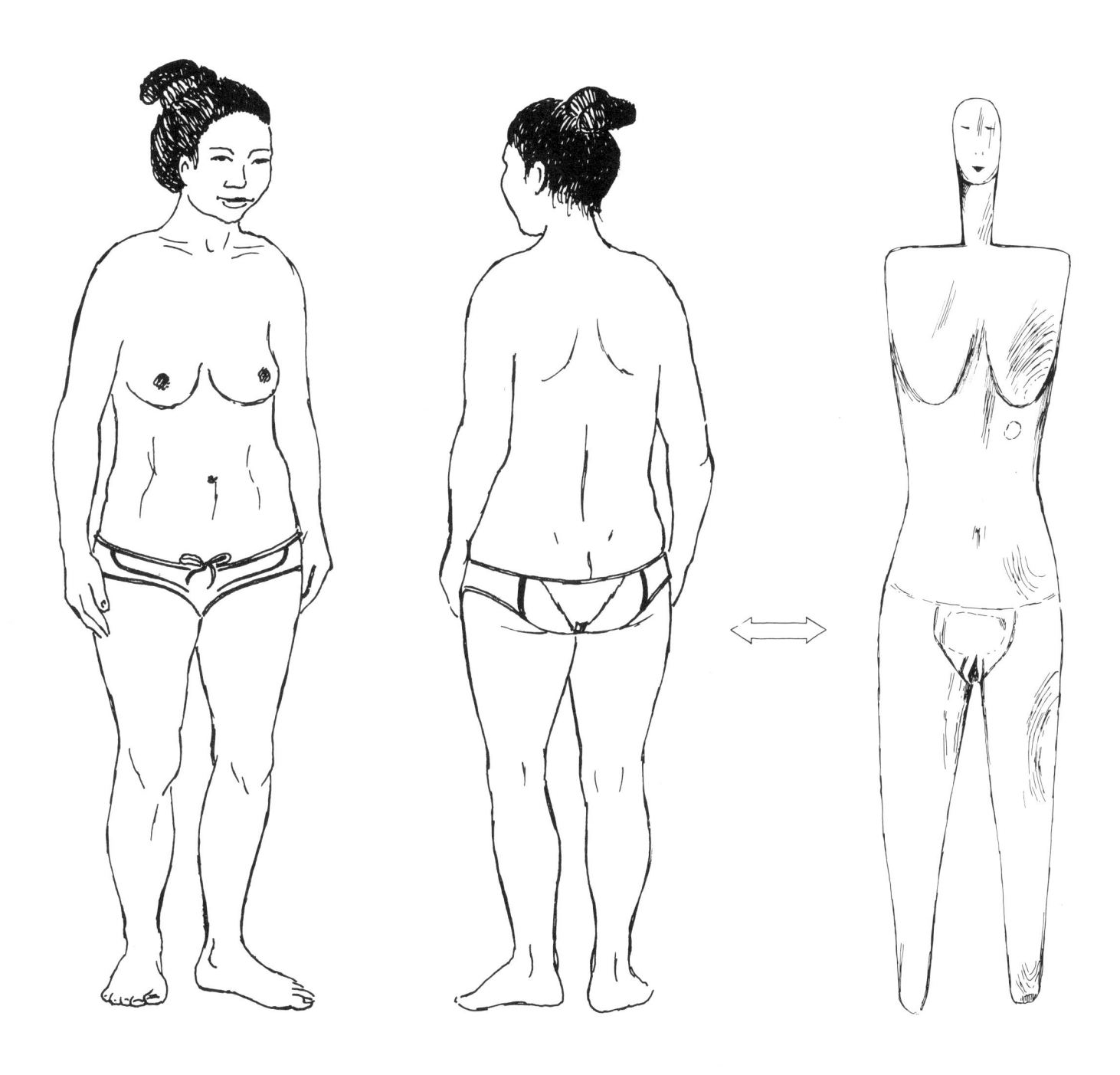

Woman in small ornamented house pants. To the right a wooden figure from North Greenland, now in the National Museum. Stylistically this can well be from the same period as the women who perished at Qilakitsoq.

These short pants, house pants, are the only clothing that adults wore indoors; children went about naked. The pants are beautifully ornamented. When the thighbone ornament for both sexes is marked on the outer pants, it is shown as a clear stripe on the thighs in front. But oddly enough it is different with the thighbone ornament on the West Greenland women's house pants, which we know from a few examples saved from earlier centuries, now in the National Museum. Here the stripes are seen over the buttocks. Between these two thighbone stripes sits a piece of the snout-skin of caribou, and to its lower tip is sewed a flap of folded skin with the fur removed. It does not take much imagination to see what this represents – a woman's sex attribute.

On the small house pants from Qilakitsoq, in spite of their present crumpled condition, it can be seen clearly that the thighbone ornamentation here as well is on the backside. But there is meanwhile another ornament on the front of the pants, namely a curved line from the hip in toward the crotch. This is the first time I have seen this ornament. Taken in relationship to the thighbone ornament on the back of the pants, there can be only one explanation, namely that the curved line is to mark the contour of the pelvis as seen from the rear. But why all this shifting back to front on the woman's pants? The explanation can only be this, that the woman is to be protected from any eventual sorcery attack against her fertility: if sorcery is practised against her, it will hit her the wrong way round, where it can do no harm – it will, so to speak, 'hit the wrong side of town.'

These little house pants' primary functional import connects with that of the amulet to such a

The lowest figure in Grave 2. Note the lower jaw which had been knocked off, and the 'bag' up by the head, eiderduck skin turned inside out. [NOTE: Later tests placed this woman, Number Eight, at about 50 years of age; her height at 150 cm or 4 feet 11 inches.]

The mouth of Umanaq Fjord at the beginning of April. Ice as far as the eye can see.

degree that one will scarcely be wrong in claiming that they are first and foremost protective amulets and only in second place articles of clothing.

For out-of-doors use women had two lengths of pants to choose from: one pair short – but longer than the house pants – and one pair long, exactly like the men's. All these pants extend from the middle of the hip to below the knee. The outer pants which could be examined so far [NOTE: as of 1979] are all of sealskin, except for the pair mentioned a while back, where the upper part was of a reddish dog fur, while the lower legs were of sealskin. Just to complete the picture it should be mentioned that the baby boy's rompers with the fur turned inward, must be made of a 3 to 4 months' old puppy. The outer pants are very simple in cut, in principle two tubes which are sewed together at the crotch. And there is no ornamental work on the thigh in front on any of them. The pants of most of the dead women are shoved down into the kamik shafts, but for the woman lowest in Grave 2, whose pant leg is pulled up to the thigh, it can be seen that the pants end in a runner band for a cord to tie them tight under the knee.

The kamiks of five of the women all are wide and roomy around the leg, but on the whole there are no two single kamiks exactly alike. One wonders a little that nothing much in the way of trimming can be seen on them. A toe piece which has been sewn on and a boat-shaped wedge patch on both of the tall woman's kamiks make a rather clumsy effect, while on the contrary all the soles apart from the top figure in Grave 2, show an expertise corresponding to the outer coats' almost over-fastidious stitching. On the edge of the kamik soles at about the middle of the foot, opposite each other, are two holes through which the kamik thong is drawn. For only a single one of the women are these holes used for their proper purpose; in one pair which had a circular band near the foot, it was simply wrapped around the ankle. At the front and the back the kamiks' seams are nicely pleated together, which gives the kamik soles a kind of decorative striping at toe and heel.

Umanaq Island seen towards the west. A day of hoarfrost fog, at the end of March.

For stockings, caribou skin is used, lengthened at the top with sealskin. The upper section of the stocking projects, in all cases but one, up over the shaft of the kamik; this seems typical for men's wear, when we take the older boy's kamiks as the norm. This means that the hunter, when he sets out through the snow in winter, has his stockings sticking out with their upper edge pulled up over his knees, and pushed in under the bottom edge of his pants, which extend to just a little below the knee. The pants are drawn tight with aid of a running band and in the same way the kamik's upper edge is firmly fastened, so everything is closed around the knee. No further protection than this is needed against the snow, which is not more than 10 centimetres deep on the ice in Umanaq Fjord.

A bundle of winter-plucked dry kamik grass lay between the top and next to top figures in Grave 2. This dried grass is inserted between the shoe sole and the stocking as a good insulation layer; it is collected below the bird cliffs in winter time when it is withered and dried through. The same thing is done today.

Taken as a whole, the Qilakitsoq mummies' apparel gives almost no impression of being worn-out. The coats and pants which it has been possible to examine more closely [NOTE: as of 1979], have no bare patches where the fur has been worn away. Only one loose-lying and very crushed coat shows evidence of wear along the edges. The soles in most cases are newly sewed on; indeed so new that they still bear some of the sheared-off fur. These new soles, having been exposed to further drying-out over the subsequent centuries, have shrunk so much that the dead people's heels have slid out of the kamik heels. But the bigger child's heels and those of one of the women have not slid out. Their kamiks were not new, and having been well treated by being worn soft and stretched, were so stabilized that they give no impression of having shrunk. The young woman with the fine teeth had on absolutely new kamiks – small tufts of cut-off fur were still stuck to the soles and sides of them. But another pair of soles had patches sewed over holes that had worn through.

The explanation for the brand-new clothes is doubtless to be sought in the tradition that the Inuit, as they neared the settlement location where they had decided to spend the winter, dressed up in absolutely new coats and pants – they were less fussy about kamiks and undershirts – and the old togs were laid aside. This was done so as not to bring poverty and misery with them to their new residence. Singing happily, wearing their shiny new furs, they intended to come paddling in to their settlement. In a word, they were off to a fresh start.

No mitts were found with the bodies. Inuit women seldom wear mitts; they pull their hands up into their sleeves or completely inside, and hold them against their bare body. Did our special Thule Eskimos meet their fate on a September day back in the 1400s when they sailed in towards their home at Qilakitsoq?

* * *

AN EXAMINATION of a group of Stone Age hunters and fisher folk's costumes cannot end without a few words, or even better a drawing, to show graphically what immense work had to be done by the hunter and no less by his wife so that they could put clothes on their bodies. The skins of all the birds and animals shown in the drawing had to be flayed, scraped free of fat and tissue, be softened and then sewn – all for one single outfit. No wonder that they went around in their old togs until by a year's end these fell off their backs.

4 to 6 fjord seals for the jacket
1 fjord seal for the pants
1 blue-side (young Greenland seal) for kamiks
⅛ black-side (adult Greenland seal) for shoe soles
1 caribou or dog skin for stockings
20 to 25 eiderduck skins for the inner shirt.

Biographical Details

JENS ROSING was born on July 28, 1925, a son of a Lutheran priest in Jakobshavn on the northwest coast of Greenland. He was actually born in the same room in which the celebrated Knud Rasmussen had seen the light of day (or night, as the case may be, that far north) forty-six years earlier. Father Otto Rosing was pastor, painter and carver in wood, who in the course of his pastoral work moved around Greenland a good deal with his family, including to the parish of Angmagssalik on the east coast, where the boy Jens had as tutor the cousin of my Greenland-1941 friend Grethe Tønnesen. (Everybody knows everybody else up in that vast land; Jens would be sixteen in 1941 and likely already at school in Denmark, but he told me his mother lived in Godthåb at that time.)

After passing his *Realeksamen* (school-leaving) Jens was enrolled for training in the Royal Greenland Trading Company in Copenhagen, but skipped out because he wanted to be an artist. In 1950 he entered the Danish Academy of Arts School for Painting, but didn't last long there either because academic accuracies bored him. He continued to draw and to write on his own, with a great feeling for folklore, especially that of his native land. Later in 1950 he headed north to Finnish Lapland, to live for two years among the Sami (as the Lapps call themselves) in order to learn their skills in handling semi-domesticated reindeer. The final stage of his two-year apprenticeship was in Norway's Finnmark, where he helped to select suitable fine specimens of the reindeer to import into Greenland, as a new experiment there in 'semi-domestication.' Subsequently he was in charge of the reindeer station at Innera in Godthåb Fjord from 1952 to 1959.

Rosing took part in several Greenland expeditions of the Danish National Museum. In May 1966 he went with his wife and four children to Egedesminde on the west coast, where he made a unique documentary colour film about '*Store Otto* – Big Otto – the last journey in the women's boat.' Subsequently Greenland's last remaining *umiak* was acquired by him for the Museum in Godthåb / Nuuk while he was Director there.

Actively engaged in ceramics as well, Rosing created the altar-piece in Egedesminde and the decorations for the historic Seminary in Nuuk. The *landsråd* (local government) commissioned him to design and execute a metal bracelet set with 'Greenland stones' for presentation to the heir to the Danish throne on the occasion of a visit to Greenland. In 1982 there appeared the handsome series of commemorative stamps he designed to celebrate the thousandth anniversary of the Norsemen's arrival in Greenland under fearsome Erik the Red. The *Berlingske Times* art critic, Eichner-Larsen, is said to have described the set as 'one of the best in the entire northern hemisphere.... The whole series is studded with elements from Greenland's flora, fauna and everyday life, as well as ancient Inuit culture – *taget nøjagtig på kornet*, caught accurately on the wing (or on the nose?) – by the hand of the huntsman

Rosing. He is completely at home with the world of his subjects.' (From an article by Lilot in *Berlingske Tidende* in July 1985.)

It was equally natural for Jens Rosing to combine his love of local lore and legend in books written and illustrated by his own hand, such as *Den dragende Flok – Herd on the move*, and *Islom – Loon*. (*Islom / Tekst og Tegninger* Jens Rosing. Grafodan Offset, Vaerløse 1980. 850 numbered copies.) It contains some poetic, graphically illustrated theorizing that the streamlined shape of the loon was first inspiration for that of the Eskimo kayak. Recently there appeared his book of east coast legends and myths: *Sagn og saga (Story and saga)* with graphics by Sven Havsteen-Mikkelsen, Rhodos Publishing House. At present a work is underway about the narwhal, whose extraordinary single projecting tusk with its elegant spiral 'fluting' was, according to Rosing, the source of the fabulous Unicorn in medieval Europe. 'Unicorn horns' were one of the Greenland-dwelling Norsemen's main objects of export in their time; the Rosings' home in Humlebaek had several of them lying here and there on the floor – left behind by unicorns, perhaps.

In 1980 Jens Rosing was awarded the Danish Authors' Association prize for popular science, likely in part on the basis of *Himlen er lav* of the previous year. Homage was paid to his 'finest scientific expertise in Eskimology.' This helps complete our introductory encirclement of the productive author-illustrator who also happened to be Director of the Greenland Museum from 1976 to 1978, just at the period when the country was working out its first phase of independence from Denmark. A remark somewhere in Rosing's text mentions that the museum was in the early 1970s 'in a considerable state of chaos,' which helps explain why nothing was done about the Inuit find from 1972 until 1977 when the Grønvold brothers made another attempt to have professional attention paid to their extraordinary discovery. We can be thankful that is was Jens Rosing to whom they now came.

Naomi Jackson Groves

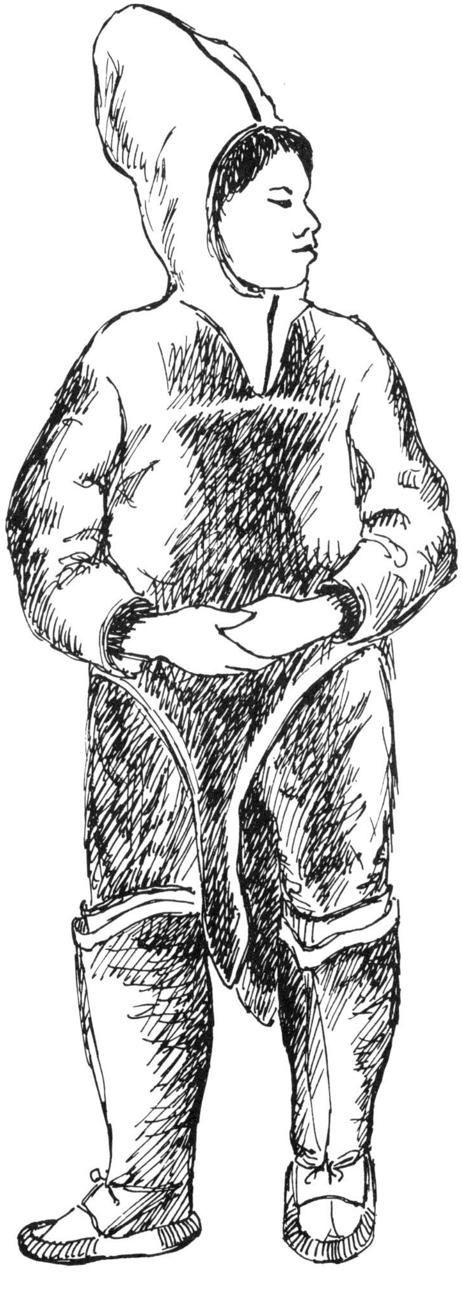